# Double Black

## A Stark Springs Academy Novel

### Book 2

### By Ali Dean

# Chapter 1

Unstoppable. That's how I feel as my burning muscles press into the final turn of the training run. Tucking low, I zoom through the last stretch as if it's a real race, grinning despite heavy breathing and frigid weather. It's only nine in the morning, single-digit temperatures, and we've been on the slopes for two hours. Still, when my alarm went off at six this morning, I had no desire to stay curled up in my warm bed. The ski season is halfway over, and I've gone from a potential mistake at Stark Springs Academy, an underdog, to the newest threat in town. It. Feels. Awesome. And it didn't come without some serious head games.

Snapping out of my skis and heading into the training hut, I know this is only the beginning. Sure, I've had one killer race that put me on the podium and got my name buzzing around in the ski world, but if I don't jump on, hold tight, and ride with this momentum, I'll just be that girl who had that one great race.

"Looks like someone had a good morning training." Ryker's voice wraps me in warmth, and I sigh, happy I don't have to resist the effect he has on me anymore.

He's sitting on a bench by my locker, taking off his snowboarding boots.

"How could you tell? You couldn't see us from the half-pipe, could you?" I like that Ryker has an alpine skiing background, even though he decided on a different sport. It means we can speak the same language. He understands my world. Probably even better than I do, actually.

He stands up and walks me backward until my back is pressed to my locker.

"You're actually walking with a bounce, which is no easy feat wearing ski boots. Your eyes are shiny. Your cheeks are flushed. And you were smiling even before you saw me."

"Even before I saw you, huh?"

He lowers his head, a slight smile of his own playing on his lips, like he's got a secret. "You always smile when you see me, even when you try not to." Ryker seems embarrassed to admit this, which is cute, since it's probably me who should be embarrassed. Still, this means he noticed me, even when he was pretending to ignore me.

He's not ignoring me anymore though, and I can feel his eyes roaming over me as I tug my feet out of my ski boots and slide sweatpants on over my training GS suit.

"It's been three days, Roxanne," he murmurs. "Have you decided?"

I glance up at him as I exchange my helmet for a winter hat. "Yup."

His eyebrows rise skeptically. "Oh?"

Shutting my locker, I take his hand, thankful that we can enjoy these gestures of affection without worrying about who will see us and what it means. "Give me a ride back to DH?" The dining hall on the Stark Springs Academy campus is open all day, and my stomach is demanding breakfast. My second breakfast of the day, sure, but we work out first thing each morning and this girl needs her fuel.

Our hands remain locked together as we walk from the Stark training hut to Ryker's pickup. He's waiting for me to tell him what I want to do about Petra Hoffman, Aspen Davies and Winter Lovett, the three girls who left me stranded in the woods, at night, in a blizzard. On purpose.

He's pulling out of the resort parking lot when I tell him.

"I don't want you to do anything to them except what's already done."

Ryker's brow furrows, and I know this isn't what he wanted to hear from me.

"But nothing's been done." He knows it isn't true, even as he says it.

"They lost their precious posse status, Ryker. They no longer have the respect or the notoriety or whatever that they were so desperate for in the first place. You know that's why they did that to me, don't you?"

"Because you threatened them. In more ways than one."

"Because I didn't respect their rules. *Your* rules. The Stark hierarchy." I don't say it maliciously, though there's a bite in my tone. How can there not be? It's what divided us from the very beginning.

"But Roxanne, I told you, I'm willing to change the way things are, if that's what you want. So if it's all changing anyway, how is it any form of punishment to strip the girls of their social power?"

Ryker isn't stupid. Actually, he's probably too smart for his own good most of the time. But when it comes to high school social life, he's a little clueless.

"If you aren't behind them at school, that will suck. If you aren't behind them when they graduate, it will suck even more. It's more of a long-term, slow pain, than a quick one right to the gut. Know what I mean?" For girls like Petra Hoffman, being someone who matters is everything. Taking that away is the ultimate punishment for girls who care too much about being in the spotlight.

Ryker still isn't buying it. He's getting there, but he wants a revenge or a punishment, as he called it, that's cut and dry. One that inflicts pain immediately and is a clear "eye for an eye" type of response for what they did.

"You're the one who once told me that Petra wanted it all. She doesn't just want to be the fastest alpine skier at Stark, or even in the world. She wants to be the biggest, a household name, famous everywhere."

He's nodding now, and I know I've got him.

"In order to get there," he fills in, "she needs more than Aspen and Winter as her allies."

"She needs *you* to get what she wants, Ryker. And she needs Stark behind her. The school, the team, its name, and the people here. She's going to lose all of that. She already has. We don't need to do anything else besides keep her out. Don't let her back in." It's cruel, in a way, but not really. She wants too much, as far as I'm concerned, and in the end, none of it should even matter. It was her unchecked ambition and jealousy that had me lost in the middle of nowhere in a snowstorm. Aspen and Winter share some of Petra's ambition, or they put their faith in the wrong girl, followed along when they shouldn't have. They all knew exactly what they were doing when they sped away on their snowmobiles.

"That's it?" Ryker asks, glancing over at me.

"That's it."

"Okay, then."

"Okay? It's done?"

"I'll tell the guys, and Telly, but yeah, that's it."

"What about Telluride? What will she do? Weren't those girls her best friends?" Telluride Valentini will be the only other girl in the "posse" now. The posse is basically just a silly name for the most popular group at Stark, but, like everything at Stark, it's more exclusive and elite than a typical high school social circle. The members aren't just cool and gorgeous like most popular people, but they are all captains of their teams, which are some of the best teams in the world. Though the group changes each school year, it's well-defined.

"I've talked to her. She wasn't involved and didn't know what they were up to. And you say she never did anything else to you, right?"

"No, Telluride never gave me a hard time." It's true. The senior hockey star is intimidating, that's for sure, but she didn't seem to care enough to worry about me.

"Then nothing will change for her," Ryker says decidedly. At the beginning of the school year I would have assumed that it didn't matter to Ryker one way or the other whether he remained friends with Telluride. I assumed he was too cold and aloof to care. But now I can read him better, and there's relief in his tone.

Telluride Valentini is the only one of his friends who was born in Stark Springs, like he was. Though Petra Hoffman moved here when she was ten years old, Telly and Ryker have been friends forever.

"I know, but doesn't this mean she's losing her friends? The guys might not care as much, but won't it suck for her? It will seem like a punishment when she didn't do anything."

Ryker shakes his head. "No. Telly wasn't crazy about Petra, Winter or Aspen. She's closer with the posse girls who graduated last year and with her hockey teammates."

"Was she in the posse last year?"

"Yes."

It's weird hearing Ryker talk about the posse, acknowledging its existence. Of course he knows what it is and what it stands for, but he's finally willing to talk about it with me in a way he hadn't been before.

"Maybe there shouldn't *be* a posse anymore, Ryker. Then Telly can just hang out with her hockey friends whenever, and with you and the guys whenever. Why does it need to be this official group?"

Ryker pulls into the parking lot outside DH. He's frowning when he turns to face me, and I think I've rattled him. "But then, who's in charge? What about order and leadership? And how about what you said about the girls who hurt you? If there isn't any posse, then they don't lose as much. There needs to be incentive."

"Those girls still won't get respect here. And you and others won't give them the support they need to get on the right teams after Stark, the best sponsorships, all that stuff, right?" He's nodding, but his frown is deepening. "And Ryker, Stark isn't a business and the posse isn't the governing board. That might be the world you know how to function in, but this is just high school. Order and leadership mean something different here."

I hope I haven't taken it too far too soon. But someone has to get through to this boy. He might be eighteen years old and a man by most standards, but he jumped right over a few formative years, and I think he lost part of himself when he did. Ryker's mom died when he was twelve, and he became an adult over the next couple of years, taking over Stark, Inc. as a teenager.

"I don't know if I can agree with you on that, Roxanne," he finally says. "Stark isn't like other high schools. But I told you I'd change. I made that promise. And I'm willing to try doing things your way, if it means you'll trust me, and stay with me." His words sound far too thought-out and mature for a high school junior, but I've learned that doesn't mean he's indifferent. It isn't easy for him to concede like this. His willingness to listen to me and accept my opinions means everything.

My hand reaches out to his jaw, holding it, letting him know that I understand. I'm not throwing his words back at him, or trying to take advantage of whatever influence I seem to have on him.

"You coming in or just dropping me off?" I murmur.

"I've got class. I'll see you at DH for dinner, and I'll let people know the rules are changing."

"No, not changing. No rules at all."

I can almost feel his heart seizing. He doesn't know how to function in a world without rules. "Okay, but in my head, the non-rules are still rules. Does that work?"

Is Ryker Black making fun of himself? Acknowledging he's got some issues?

I offer him a smile and nod in agreement. Yes, I understand your crazy way of seeing the world, Ryker Black. I try to convey it by leaning forward, tracing my thumb along his lower lip.

"Are you going to kiss me now, or what?" I ask.

He flashes me the smile with dimples, the one that still catches me off guard and makes my insides tremble. Ryker whispers, "Your demands never stop, do they, Roxanne?" But he doesn't mind this one. No, he's happy to give me the kiss I want. And then some.

# Chapter 2

"I want you to know," Player Westby says as he slides into the chair next to me, "that I have been rooting for you since day one."

DH is nearly empty, but I know it still matters that a member of the posse is sitting with me. Not that it should, and not that it will going forward, since the posse is going to disband and all that, but still, Player Westby is hot stuff around these parts. He was winning world snowboarding competitions in the seventh and eighth grades, and even though I hadn't heard of him before I came to Stark, he was famous in the snowboarding world. He didn't do as well over the next couple of years, but is back on the podium again this year.

Oh, and he's one of Ryker Black's best friends. So there's that.

"Rooting for me? What does that mean exactly? And are you eating Lucky Charms mixed with fro yo?"

He grins. "Want a bite?"

"Next time."

He shrugs. "I've always been Team Roxie Slade. I wanted you to be friends with us."

"You mean it wasn't all up to Ryker?"

He chuckles. "Not with you, Slade. He wanted you. *We* wanted you, except for maybe Petra," he says with a wink. "But you didn't want us. Not at first. So, really, it was up to you."

"I didn't know you. I only didn't want to be your friend because Ryker was an asshole about it and acted like I had no say."

"Fair enough. But just for the record, if Ryker hadn't threatened my life, I would've hung out with you from day one. Cody too, and probably Sven, though maybe not, since Petra had him wrapped around her finger for a while there."

I'm assuming he's speaking figuratively about Ryker's threat, but I'm not going to ask. It's water under the bridge, or whatever.

"Sven's been acting like a body guard at practice. Ingrid too. They need to chill out." They think Petra might try something on me, but I disagree. Like I explained to Ryker, she's got no power and hurting me will gain her nothing.

Player ignores that comment. "Yeah, it's good for Sven to have a new reason to be angry with Petra. She went out with him last year and then Ryker showed some interest in her and she totally ditched Sven to try to get Ryker's attention. And then you showed up, and well, no other girl stood a chance."

I almost choke on my orange juice. It wasn't really like that, was it? Is it?

"Anyway," he goes on, like he isn't shaking me all up with his words, "we're going to be friends from here on out, but just know, I will never hit on you."

"Uh, yeah, okay, Player." His name is *actually* Player. It's not even a nickname, though it's incredibly accurate, given his reputation.

"I'm just saying, don't interpret our friendship like that. I want to keep my balls, thank you very much, and I like you and want us to be cool, but you and me, we're going to have a nice clear understanding. No matter what I say or how I say it, I am not meaning to hit on you. Sometimes I just get that way with a pretty girl."

"Right, so like how you just called me pretty?"

"Exactly," he says with a wink, and I think I know just what he's getting at.

I laugh and shake my head.

"Isn't this cute?" Petra's voice cuts through my laughter. She looks between us with a smirk. "Ryker will be thrilled to hear how well you two are getting along."

"What do you want, Petra?" Players asks tiredly.

"I want to know what Ryker is planning, and when he's going to do it so we can go back to normal. It's been three days since he found out and so far he's just ignored us."

Aspen appears from behind her then, and I'm not really sure where she came from. The blonde snowboarder glares at me. "Maybe he just doesn't care enough about what we did to Roxie to do anything about it," she suggests.

"Or, maybe, he's leaving it up to me to decide," I retort.

Both girls blink, taken aback. Petra's eyes narrow after a moment. "Is that true, Player?"

Player leans back in his chair and takes a slow bite of his Lucky Charms concoction. "Yep."

The color begins to drain from Petra's face while Aspen's cheeks redden in anger. Aspen doesn't address me, instead asking Player, "Don't you think that's a problem, Player? Who's this girl to decide what to do? She's no one. Her parents work at a little country store in the middle of nowhere."

It's nothing I haven't heard already since arriving at Stark six months ago, but it's still upsetting. The truth is, I do feel like an outsider at times, when most people in Ryker's circles come from prominence. I even felt like an outsider at Sugarville, my home mountain. My parents grew up in the same town I grew up in, Ashfield, Vermont, but they weren't part of the skiing community.

Player is unconcerned by his teammate's outburst. "So? She kicked Petra's ass at the Beaver Creek Carnival, didn't she? But it doesn't even matter. Ryker says Roxie decides, and that's that."

Petra's regained herself. She speaks sternly. "What about you, Player? You're going to let your best friend act stupid over *her*?" Petra flicks her hand in my direction.

"If I were you, I'd be nice to her." Player leans forward, talking quietly. "Your fate is in her hands." The words hit me, if only because Ryker said something similar to me on my first day here.

*"The only unwavering rule is that I'm holding your future in the palm of my hand."*

Petra scoffs. "I don't think so. I've spent the last eight years getting to know Ryker Black and earning his trust. We hurt her *for him*. And he's going to realize that."

Aspen isn't listening to her friend. She's looking right at me. "Well? What do you want him to do to us?"

It's like they finally decided I'm worth acknowledging, but I can see the reluctance to accept it, even as Aspen asks the question.

"Nothing," I say simply. "We're done with you. That's it."

Aspen frowns, confused, but Petra takes a step back like I've smacked her. She gets it. Aspen reaches for Petra's arm, opens her mouth to say something, but then closes it.

Player fake-punches me playfully on the arm. "I like it."

His approval is like a nail in the coffin. It says that he never wanted them in the first place, that it doesn't hurt him to see them go. Three of the girls he's spent most of high school hanging out with are out of his life with my words, and all he can say is that he likes it. He doesn't demand a punishment that would allow them to earn back their places in the posse. He's ready for them to be done, too.

"But, the posse? It can't change now." Petra, on the other hand, is unwilling to accept it.

"Yeah, it's not like Roxie and her friends are posse material. What? Telly's going to be the only girl? Ryker won't like that." Aspen's starting to get what this means, and she won't believe it.

"There's not going to be a stupid posse," I say dismissively. Petra actually gasps at my irreverence. "And before you go off about it, Ryker already knows." As of twenty minutes ago, but still, he agreed. "He doesn't want things to be like they always have," I add at the girls' shocked expressions. It might be pushing the truth, since what Ryker really wants is me, and he's only willing to change to get that, but whatever.

Petra shoots Player a meaningful look, like, *See? This girl is crazy!* And I force myself not to glance at him to check his reaction. I need him on my side. Well, no, I really only need Ryker, but it will be easier if Player and the other guys go along with it.

"Like I told Roxie earlier, I've always been on her side. And I was right. She's full of good ideas. Glad Ryker finally figured it out."

I try really hard to fight my grin, but it breaks free.

Petra's entire body is rigid as she shakes her head in disgust. "Come on, Aspen, let's go."

The two turn to leave and practically run over Ingrid Koller, my closest friend on the ski team at Stark.

"What was that about?" she asks as she sits at our table. I like that she doesn't hesitate. Ingrid has handled the revelation about Ryker as my boyfriend and the newfound interaction with the, er, non-posse, fairly smoothly. My roommate Monica Danvers is still suspicious about the whole thing, as far as I can tell. She doesn't trust any of it. I can't blame her, after her best friend Olga Popova got kicked out of Stark for stepping on the posse's toes.

Player tells her, "Roxie's in charge now, and the princesses don't like it."

Ingrid pauses with her toast midair, halfway to her mouth, but I think I'm even more shocked by Player's announcement and at the realization that he's right. Ryker has to agree with whatever I propose, but in essence, yeah, he handed over the reins. I'm the new boss at Stark, whether I asked for it or not.

The news about the princesses' demise travels fast. People don't know the reasons behind it, not exactly, but they seem to have caught wind that my position has elevated, if the lingering stares mean anything. And they aren't stares of disapproval, but something else. Awe and admiration? Maybe. I'd like to think it's from my accomplishments on the slope over the weekend, but I didn't notice the change until after the DH episode this morning.

I'm doing leg lifts in the weight room after classes when Ryker finds me. I haven't seen him since this morning, and I don't know whether he'll like how I handled Petra and Aspen. But when he sees me, he comes right over and leans in for a kiss. Just a little one, but it tells me things are fine.

"Come over for dinner tonight, after this?" He's not really asking, but I don't mind. I'm happy to escape another DH scenario. "I'm ordering Mario's and Telly and the guys are coming."

"Oh, okay, cool." So we're hanging out with all his friends. The non-posse. I don't mind, but what about *my* friends? "Can I invite Ingrid?"

"Yeah, of course," he says easily. "Sorry, I should have said so."

He's trying to do this right, and I know it's not easy for him. This isn't a business merger or takeover, though I know that's what his mind wants to make it.

"Invite whomever you'd like, Roxanne," he adds.

But I don't want to invite Monica, and so I don't. She needs to get over her fears if we're going to continue being friends. Her boyfriend, Liam Briarwell, and Liam's roommate, Misha Vans, are my friends as well, but Monica's friends first. I don't want to cause a rift with anyone, but I also need to just do what feels comfortable, and not force anything or overthink it. Besides, Ingrid's right here in the weight room with me while Monica, Liam and Misha are at figure skating practice over at the rink.

Ingrid doesn't question me about it when I invite her. She's been pretty determined to be at my side since finding out about what the princesses did to me. She didn't scold me for not telling her in the first place, or warn me about dating Ryker, or give any other unwanted opinions. That's the kind of friend I need right now.

Sven Teslow, the captain of the guys' ski team, gives us a ride over to Ryker's after we shower and change in the gym locker rooms. Our dorms are only a short walk away, but when it's freezing cold it's nice to minimize walking. Which is ridiculous, given how much time we spend on the mountain, but hey, I guess it's no different than people who drive around for parking spots ten feet closer to fitness centers. Ryker's got a dorm room, but he rarely uses it since the home he grew up in is only a few minutes from campus. His mother died over five years ago and his father is usually off traveling or at one of their other homes, so he normally has the place to himself.

We pull up behind a Land Rover in Ryker's driveway and Ingrid asks, "Isn't that Winter's car?"

Sven eyes it before confirming with a nod. "She shouldn't be here."

My stomach churns with unease. The confrontation with Aspen and Petra at DH this morning more than met my quota of drama for the day. I'm not up for another round.

"This will be fun," Ingrid comments, heavy on the sarcasm.

Sven glances over at me as we walk to the front door. He looks... concerned. Have I not already proven that I've got tough skin?

"Don't worry. I can handle the princesses." It's what I've taken to calling Winter Lovett, Aspen Davies and Petra Hoffman. Player dubbed them that first this morning, but I'm running with it.

Ingrid glances behind her with a smirk. "Careful, the princesses have teeth."

"More like fangs," Sven murmurs.

Don't I know it.

# Chapter 3

The house is eerily quiet when we step inside the main foyer. Turning the corner to the kitchen, we walk into a silent standoff between the princesses and the rest of the former posse. Player Westby stands by Cody Tremblay, the boys' hockey team captain, leaning against the counter. Telluride Valentini sits perched on a bar stool, arms crossed, glaring at Petra, Winter and Aspen, who huddle together on the other side of the kitchen island. Ryker is nowhere in sight.

I know in this moment that it's up to me to step forward.

"What are you doing here?" I'm relieved my voice doesn't shake.

My eyes remain steadily trained between Winter, Aspen and Petra, but I can feel everyone in the kitchen looking at me now. I'm the least connected person in this room, as far as my ties to the winter sports world go, but for this instant, I'm the leader.

"We need to talk to Ryker," Petra replies.

"You weren't invited." At least, I don't think they were. I just saw Ryker at the gym, and he would have told me.

"That's none of your business," Aspen says, taking a hesitant step forward. She wants to stand against me, but she's nervous.

I cross my arms and lift my chin. "It is. I explained it this morning and I don't want to repeat myself. He's done with you." I circle a finger around. "*We* are done with you. And it could be worse. So really, just let it go."

Ingrid speaks up then. "You should be thanking Roxie. After what you did to her, she could've retaliated with something that took you out for the rest of the season, or worse. Losing your status at Stark and your friendships, if you can even call them that, with the posse, is nothing. You shouldn't be here."

Go Ingrid. I try to hide my surprise at her confident declarations.

I notice the eyes in the kitchen drift to the stairs, and my gaze follows. Ryker takes us in as he descends the staircase. He's wearing dark jeans, a Stark hoodie, and his chestnut hair is still wet from a shower. His casual attire contrasts with the look on his face. Ryker is pissed, and even though I know I'm not the recipient of that anger, it still sends a chill through me.

He doesn't say anything when he walks into the kitchen and over to me, taking my hand in his. "What are they doing here, Roxanne?" he asks darkly. But his question tells everyone who's in charge. Me.

"I was just asking them the same question. They weren't invited."

He tilts his head to the side, trying to decide how to handle it.

Winter speaks up then. "Ryker, we need to talk to you. This silent treatment is stupid. We know that you didn't approve of the stunt we pulled with Roxie, but that was months ago. You found out three days ago and we've heard nothing from you. We'll take a punishment, we're ready for it." Her voice isn't confident, and when Ryker turns around to face her, it begins to shake. "Did you know what Roxie told Petra and Aspen this morning? That's not true, is it?"

"What'd she tell them?" he asks. I'm pretty sure he already knows but he wants to hear them say it.

Petra squares her shoulders. "That she decides our punishment, and that there won't be one. Only that you're done with us."

Aspen scoffs. "And that there's no more posse."

Ryker shrugs, like it doesn't matter to him. Like *they* don't matter to him. He doesn't give away whether or not I talked to him about it, or if this is the first he's hearing of it. "If that's what Roxie decided, then that's that."

Sven adds, "I think that means you should get out."

The girls shuffle their feet uncertainly. Winter starts to back away but Aspen grabs her arm. "No. No way. We're not letting *her*, this *nobody*, push us out. Let's talk about this, Ryker. Guys, what we did was a smart move. Things went back to normal once she went away." Aspen looks around at the others, trying to gain their support.

Cody laughs, but there's little humor behind it. "How stupid are you? Things did not go back to normal. And our normal is whack anyway. Ryker was upset." Cody realizes his words may have gone too far only after he's said them. "Sorry, man," he adds, but Ryker doesn't stop him. "He didn't know what the three of you did to Roxie, but he wasn't happy because she wasn't around anymore. You got in the middle of him and Roxie when you shouldn't have. You had no right."

"We were looking out for him," Petra argues. "She's white trash. She might be fast on skis, sometimes, but she'll screw it all up. She's not like us."

I feel Ryker twitching beside me, and I take comfort in his anger. It's a low blow, and I can't deny that it hurts. But Player is the first to lash back.

"You're just jealous, Petra. It's plain to all of us. Roxie's good for Ryker. Hell, she's good for all of us. And she's got more class than the three of you."

What is happening here? How did this become all about me? Has it always been that way? No, this is bigger than me. Or me and Ryker. This is the start of a shift. Major changes are going to happen at Stark, and they may even have a ripple effect to other aspects of the winter sports world. Not to make it a big deal or anything, but it feels like it could be. What's happening here in the kitchen could be huge. I sense it in my chest to the tips of my toes.

There's a heavy silence for a brief instant, and I think it's time for me to say something.

"It's time to go, princesses," I tell them.

Winter's eyes bulge, Petra's jaw drops and Aspen storms away. The other two follow after a second.

"I don't think they like their new nickname," I murmur.

I hear snickering and realize it's Telluride, who hasn't said a word yet. She catches my eye, and when the door slams behind the girls, her muffled chuckles turn into full-out laughter. At least now I know where she stands on this.

"Princesses! I love it," she gasps out, and the rest of us join in. Even Ryker, though he's shaking his head.

His hand roams to my waist and he pulls me to him, lowering his head to my ear. I think he wants to say something to me, but I only feel his hot breath on my neck.

The doorbell rings, and we all look at each other in confusion. Back so soon? And why would they ring the doorbell?

I feel Ryker's chest rise and fall behind me in laughter, and then his hand slips away.

"It's just Mario's, guys," he tells us before walking away to get the door.

We all sag with relief but when we hear the delivery guy tell Ryker he almost got pummeled by three crazy chicks in the front walkway, we burst into laughter again.

It feels good. It feels like we've gotten over a huge hurdle. And I don't mean getting rid of the princesses. I mean the reshuffling of loyalties and acceptance of my place, which, I guess, is at Ryker's side. His friends are cool with me, and it's not going to be awkward.

Telluride hops down from her barstool and walks over to me. She opens her arms for a hug. "Come here. You are my new favorite person."

Or maybe I spoke too soon. It's just a little awkward when the captain of the girls' hockey team embraces me like we're old friends. Telly is six feet of solid muscle, and radiates an intimidation factor even when she's smiling.

"Thank you for getting rid of those girls. I wasn't sure I could put up with them until graduation without snapping."

Oh. Wow. Okay, then.

The guys speak out their agreements.

Telluride points to Sven. "You only got over your thing for Petra a few months ago, buddy. Remember when you were panting after her? You thought she walked on water."

Cody says, "Yeah man, I hated how you always defended her snobby attitude."

Sven isn't fazed by the insults as he reaches to open the fridge and pull out a case of beer. "Sorry, guys. She's hot and we had great hook-ups for a while there. Plus she's skiing royalty, and what can I say? That does it for me."

Player punches him on the bicep, and Sven cringes. "*Did* it for me, I mean. It just took me a while to see past my infatuation. Give a guy a break, all right? I've seen the light now."

His admission about skiing royalty makes my stomach twist. Petra's father coaches the National Ski Team, and her mother is an Olympic gold medalist in the Giant Slalom and Super-G. She grew up in Germany, where her mother is from, but moved here at age ten when her father, a dual American-German citizen, began coaching the National Team. Even without Stark behind her, she'll always continue to be skiing royalty. It's in her blood.

I'm not usually a drinker, but I snag one of the beers from the kitchen island. Petra's words about white trash linger, even though I know they shouldn't bother me. I've proven myself on the slopes, and that's all that should matter. But the truth is, even back at Sugarville, my home mountain in Vermont, there was always a shadow lurking, reminding me that I didn't quite belong. I'd nearly forgotten about it, let it fade away, until I came to Stark.

Ryker places three pizza boxes and several bags of food on the island. "I got a few pasta dishes and salads, too," he says, glancing at me. He looks like he's going to say something else, but he stops himself. I frown, and he nudges one of the containers my way. It's labeled "chicken parm" and a strange tingling rushes through me. I'm thrilled and touched that he knows my favorite dish, the one I've ordered each time I've been to Mario's, and I'm also a little freaked out. I've gotten over his ability to know every detail; it's the fact that he's used his resources to learn trivial details about me that gets me. Ryker Black certainly has more important things to do with his time.

Or maybe it was just a lucky guess. He leans over and murmurs in my ear, "I saw you eating that when you were there with your friends over Thanksgiving. And we had pizza last night, so I thought you might want something different."

His words are just what I needed to hear. So he's not weirdly investigating my eating preferences, he just noticed before and remembered. He was being thoughtful, and I shouldn't overanalyze it. It's just hard to separate who he is and what he can do from this boy who only wants to be my, er, boyfriend. I don't think we've said it aloud yet, but I'm pretty sure that's what this is.

The group hangs in the kitchen, eating dinner, chatting about nothing important, and some of us drink beer. It's nice. Easy and comfortable, even. Almost like when my friends from Vermont came to visit and we all hung out together, but now we don't have that buffer, and it's fine. Probably because the princesses are out of the picture, and I can only hope it was that easy. Something tells me they'll continue to be a nuisance, but I can handle that.

Ryker stays beside me, constantly touching me in some way, but now he steps away to take a phone call. He puts a finger up as he walks down the hallway toward the study.

"It's probably business," Telluride tells me, noticing my gaze.

"Does he get that a lot?" I'm not even sure what my question means. I mean, he's the CEO of Stark, Inc., so obviously he takes phone calls all the time. It's just, now that I think about it, he's never done that when I've been with him before.

"Oh yeah, all the time," she says. "I mean, he delegates as much as he can, but he's constantly plugged in. He has to be. I don't know how he manages to stay here at Stark and keep everything running like he does."

Sven leans forward, his elbows on the counter. "He does travel a lot. As soon as snowboard season wraps up, he'll probably be gone for a few weeks."

Wait. What? It makes sense though, even as regret chips away at the warm feelings that have taken root in my chest over the past few days. All those months when he was here for training, and we wasted them over a misunderstanding. I leave next week for three weeks in Europe, and when I get back, the competition season will be nearly over for both of us, and he'll have to travel for work. How in the world did either of us think we could have a normal relationship?

Only moments ago it seemed like everything was falling into place, and now it feels completely hopeless. I have the sudden urge to throw something and stomp my foot, like a child who was given the toy she always wanted and then had it taken away with no explanation.

Instead, I chug the rest of my beer and reach for another. It's a teenager version of a temper tantrum, I do realize this, even as I pop the cap and take a healthy gulp. And the irony doesn't escape me that Ryker is off in his study, being more of an adult than I can even imagine.

# Chapter 4

An hour goes by and Ryker still hasn't returned. Two hours later, and Sven says he's heading back to campus. Ingrid looks at me. "You coming?"

I shake my head. No. I probably should leave with them, but I'm on the couch now, and getting up seems like a lot of work. Cody started a fire, and it's warm and cozy in here. We can hear the wind whistling around outside, and I'd rather not face it. I'm a little buzzed, too. Maybe even drunk.

Ingrid glances around at the others in the room, seeking their opinion on my decision to stay. After a beat, Telluride says, "We can always bring her back, if Ryker has to keep working."

"Or I can stay here." The others don't respond at first. Should I not have said that?

"All right, come on Ingrid," Sven says, throwing an arm around her. "Let's get home and get some sleep before practice tomorrow."

I watch them go, wondering if there's more to Sven's gesture. Could he be interested in Ingrid? And would that be a good thing? They're the same height, probably 5'8" or so, but as they walk away, I see them together, and it looks right. Hmmm…

My head swings back around when they close the door, and I find Cody studying me from his spot by the fire. "Your friend is cool. Ingrid Koller. I'd never really talked to her before."

I nod, and as I do, I realize that yes, I am a little bit tipsy. And the vans to the mountain leave at 6:15 for practice tomorrow morning. What am I doing?

"Yeah. She's cool now. I wasn't so sure for a while there," I admit.

Cody asks, "What do you mean?"

I know I wouldn't be saying any of this if I hadn't been drinking, but it spills out. "She was scared of you guys. I didn't think she had the balls to stand up to you or have my back after what the princesses did. But she's come around."

Telluride leans back in an armchair, her beer resting on her knee. "You have to admit, she was probably right to be scared. I mean, look at what those girls did to you, right?" She shakes her head.

I sigh. "Yeah, I thought I might die. You know, at the time I didn't think about avalanches, just about the cold. But that would've been a way to go, huh? Like, what if I got buried in an avalanche, and the princesses never told anyone what they did? They wouldn't have found my body until all the snow melted in the summer. Messed up, right?"

Telluride sits up quickly, jostling her beer. Cody lets out a harsh chuckling sound, but it turns into a cough. "That's fucked up," he gets out eventually.

Player scoots closer to me on the couch and rests a hand around my shoulder. "Are you sure you don't want to do something more serious to those girls? When you put it like that, I mean, that's like attempted murder. We could ruin their lives if you wanted."

"Aren't we?" I ask.

"Back off, Player," Ryker grumbles as he walks into the room, though I don't think there's much emotion behind it. No, Player explained himself to me this morning, and I'm sure Ryker knows his friend better than I do. Player's just a touchy-feely dude, but he's loyal to Ryker.

Player slides away. "What do you guys think?" he asks Telly and Cody. "We should head back to the dorms and crash, huh?" It's barely 9 PM, but Stark athletes go to bed early, especially at this point in the season. We all work out several hours a day, and are usually up for practice before the sun rises, no matter our sport.

The three of them say their goodbyes, not bothering to ask if I need a ride, now that Ryker's here. As soon as we have the house to ourselves, he's by my side on the couch. I still haven't moved from my cozy spot, and a fleece blanket is wrapped around me.

"I like you here, looking so comfortable like this. You should move in."

Um, what? Even with my hazy brain at the moment, I realize his words are a big deal. Ryker doesn't say things flippantly. And since I'm not ready to address what he said, I ignore it.

"What was the call about?"

"It was Jeffrey Davies and Susan Lovett," he tells me.

"Aspen's dad and Winter's mom?"

He nods. "They conference-called me together."

"It wasn't about..." My voice drifts. Surely, the girls' parents wouldn't call Ryker about social status things like the posse. I mean, I know it's all connected, because of Ryker and who he is, but still.

"Yeah, it was about their daughters getting cut off from me. You've heard of Davies Rides, right?"

"Yeah, the snowboarding company based in California. Aspen's dad started it."

"Yeah, and Jeffrey Davies has his hands in some other pots too. Susan Lovett is the principal shareholder of Lovett Skates. You've probably never heard of them," he says, when I show no sign of recognition, "but they've been the leading figure skate designer for seventy years. Most elite figure skaters have custom Lovett skates. Anyway, they're both on the board for Stark, Inc., and I have to deal with them sometimes. The Lovetts and Davieses are friends, so they teamed up to talk to me. I'm sure I'll be hearing from Dale Hoffman at some point, though he's not as pushy."

My mind spins with this information. "You mean, you just spent the last two hours on the phone dealing with parents because of my decision?"

His eyes flash with anger. "I was dealing with them because of their daughters' poor decisions."

"Fine," I grit out.

"Are you drunk?" he asks, searching my face.

"No," I lie, and his lips rise. He doesn't seem to care about the parents, and I decide to drop it. For now. "Maybe a little. I only had like, three beers, but I don't drink much. And I don't know, it's been a crazy day."

He pulls me across his lap. "It has, hasn't it? And I was dealing with other things tonight as well. I was out of touch while at the Beaver Creek Carnival over the weekend."

And that was also, partially, because of me. At least he's speaking openly with me about what he does.

"How are we going to have time for each other?" I blurt out. I feel his body tense beneath me. "I mean, I don't even know how you have time for everything you do as it is."

"I only need a few hours of sleep," he says gently, but I sense some tension there, if only because his body is beneath my own, and it's strung tight with what he's not saying.

"Elite athletes need more than a few hours' sleep," I point out.

"Let's not talk about this right now, okay? Let's go upstairs. You're going to sleep in my bed, with me, *finally*. And you will every night until you leave for Europe next week. Can you do that?"

Oh. That does sound nice. Very nice. In the past, I slept in one of the guest rooms.

But I should protest, right? "One night at a time, Black," I say, managing enough defiance to let him know he can't boss me around.

It only makes him grin as he stands up, taking me with him, carrying me as he walks up the stairs.

I could get used to this.

***

I'm alone in Ryker's bed when my phone alarm goes off at 5:45 the next morning. The smell of coffee hits me when I open his bedroom door, and I follow it down the stairs and into the kitchen. The kitchen is empty, but the pot is full, and after filling a cup for myself, I wander to the most likely spot I'll find Ryker.

He's sitting in front of two computer screens, wearing a tee shirt, sweatpants and slippers. He hasn't seen me yet and I study him from the doorway. Ryker types away, his eyes narrowed in concentration. I wonder what he's working on. The boy is wide awake, alive as he reads one screen and then scrolls over to the other, clicking on the mouse. He shakes his head a little as he reads something, and then reaches for his coffee.

It's inspiring, really. And not because my mouth is watering from the way his muscles flex, though there's that, too. No, it's exhilarating to know he's making things happen, leading and directing an entire business, from the chair he sits on. And that he did so, secretly and pretending to be his father, when he was only thirteen or fourteen years old. Ryker Black is truly something special.

A phone in the office rings, and Ryker spins his chair to the other side of the desk, turning his back to me as he clicks onto speaker.

The callers introduce themselves and where they are calling from, and I'm reminded that while it's the crack of dawn here, it's a suitable hour for a conference call on the east coast. It's two guys from New York, and one from Montreal, and they're talking about venues for the World Cup circuit next year. The alpine ski races I hope to compete at some day. It's a conversation I can actually follow, though the politics behind choosing which mountain resort town gets to host are foreign to me.

Ryker notices me when he reaches for his coffee again, and a warm smile breaks out. It melts me. For a second there, I wasn't sure if he'd be pissed I was spying on him. He gestures for me to come closer, and when I approach, he snags me around the waist and brings me to sit on his lap, kissing along my cheek and neck.

I try hard not to make any noises as the men speak on the conference call, but he's not making it easy. Someone is definitely a morning person. I can already feel him growing beneath me and I jerk my head around, eyes wide in disbelief, mouthing, "Ryker!"

He's on the phone with the World Cup planning committee and he's growing a tent in his pants. Well, it would be one if I stood up, but he's got me firmly pressed into his lap. I didn't know about this playful, naughty side of Ryker, and I kind of love it.

Wait, no, this is wrong. Right?

The torture continues for several more minutes, me squirming half-heartedly to get away while Ryker holds me still and teases me with kisses, responding every now and then to the guys on the phone. Eventually they sign off and as soon as his grip on me loosens I jump up.

"That was *so* inappropriate!" I scold him.

He chuckles. "They weren't in here with us, Roxanne." And yes, he does have a tent now. It makes me want to skip practice. Even if I don't really know what I'd do with this situation. I mean, we've only ever kissed. Sure, it's been intense, full-body-contact kissing a few times, but with him like this and the house empty, it feels like things could escalate fast. Best to get to practice. With so much else in our relationship in the air, I don't want to make it any more complicated.

Ryker stands up and takes my hand. "Come on, let's get some breakfast." Yeah, good idea.

# Chapter 5

When Ingrid and I meet Monica, Liam and Misha for lunch at DH, the familiarity of the routine is comforting. Still, a space had been growing between Monica and me for a long time, and, in some ways, I'm not sure we ever got to a point of absolute trust. Now, it feels like there's a gap between us that might never close. It's not necessarily a problem, though, just a reality.

"I'm going to be staying at Ryker's this week," I tell her, "so don't worry about me when I don't come back to the dorm."

"Oh yeah, that's cool," she says, but I hear the wariness behind it. "I mean, I figured."

The thing is, the figure skaters are on a different schedule from us anyway, and we really don't see them very often now that we're both competing and training so much. I'm not even sure how Ingrid managed to stay friends with them all these years, and as I think about it, I realize that she probably always felt like an outsider. The dynamic is shifting for all of us, not just the posse.

"Mind if I join you guys?" It's Sven, and he hovers over us holding a lunch tray.

"Go for it, dude," Liam says easily, and it's a relief he's not freaking out like his girlfriend. Monica bites her lip and scoots closer to Liam, for comfort, I guess. Maybe once she sees that the posse isn't really a thing anymore, she'll get over the anxiety she associates with them. Really, it's like a panic disorder developed when her friend Olga Popova got the boot. She thinks that any wrong move around Ryker or his friends could result in expulsion from the school, and her paranoia makes her freeze up around them.

"I like this, Roxie," Sven says with a nod in my direction. "It got old sitting with the same people every day. Besides, hockey's at practice and the snowboarders are still on the mountain, so I'd be stuck with Petra and Winter if you hadn't changed the law."

I can't tell if there's sarcasm behind his use of the word "law."
Probably not.

"So, it's true then? Petra's out?" Misha asks, eating up the gossip.

"Kind of. But there's nothing to be out of really, anyway, right
Roxie?"

"No more posse, if that what's you mean," I confirm.

Monica blinks a few times as she takes in my words. "You mean…"
She drifts off and then her mouth forms an "o" when it sinks in.
Yes, Monica, I am the big bad scary person who makes decisions
now, so if you're going to be terrified of anyone, it's me. She holds
her shock for a beat, but then her shoulders sag like a huge weight
has been lifted from them. Maybe her anxiety is gone now, with the
understanding that the rules she's so afraid of breaking might not
even exist anymore.

Ingrid points to a far corner, where Petra puts down a tray at an
empty table. Winter joins her a moment later, so neither sits alone
but it still looks lonely. They aren't accustomed to going without an
entourage, or being looked at with pity instead of envy.

For an instant, I see myself from a distance, and realize that I'm at
*that* table, pointing and laughing at people. I don't like it. Sure,
Winter and Petra weren't just bitchy to me, they put my life in
danger, and this is suitable revenge. But it feels wrong, so I turn
back around and ignore them.

I ask Ingrid and Sven questions about the races in Europe, based
on their experiences competing there in the past. The rules are
stricter than ever when we're abroad, with Lia and Rocco Moretti in
charge. The former Olympian siblings run a tight ship at
competitions, and they don't want us distracted from racing.
Though ski racers train hard and race harder, the mountain resorts
that host the big competitions are just that – resorts. For everyone
besides the racers, it's a vacation and a chance to play and party.
It's easy to get sidetracked, and, I imagine, especially easy in

Europe, where the drinking age is like, ten. Okay, maybe it's eighteen in most places, but I hear no one cares.

If it wasn't for Ryker, I'd be filled with nothing but excited anticipation for the upcoming trip. Instead, it's tainted by the knowledge that he'll be traveling around the U.S. and Canada to snowboard competitions without me. And what if he's gone on business when I return? It could be months before we see each other, only to be separated again over summer break. My heart begins to race and my head spins as these realizations settle. I'd thought about the reality for a moment last night, but it hits even harder at this moment, as if it's finally sinking in that our relationship is doomed. And not even for the reasons that initially kept us apart.

The snowboarders filter into DH at that moment, and when Ryker's eyes find mine, they narrow in concern. I wonder if he can feel the hopelessness pouring from me. He begins to walk briskly toward us but I shake my head. Not here. We need to talk, but this isn't the place for it.

I stand up, unwilling to sit any longer as my heart sinks to my stomach. With my abrupt move, the rest of the table stares at me and I'm reminded that we are supposed to be setting a precedent here. We are showing Stark that the posse doesn't exist, that it's broken up and people are sitting with whomever they like.

"I'm sorry guys, but I really need to talk to Ryker about something," I say quickly. It suddenly seems absolutely necessary that I share my revelation with him. Maybe he hasn't even realized what we're facing. It's possible we'll only see each other for brief days at a time from now until the start of our senior year in September. That's over six months away. I will be the first to attest that everything and anything can change in six months' time.

Ryker's eyes do a quick sweep of my body, as if the answer to the panic in my eyes is physically apparent. No, Ryker, I do not have a broken leg. This one's not tangible or fixable with a cast.

"Hey," I say softly, hoping to ease his worries with a tone that isn't as frantic as I feel. "Can you put off eating for a few? I want to talk to you."

The color begins to drain from his face, and I want to reassure him that it's nothing terrible. I'm not hurt and I'm not breaking up with him. But, well, the things I'm about to say could have those repercussions.

He takes my hand and pulls me away from the main area, where I'm sure everyone is watching, down a hallway to a private room that I didn't know existed. It's a smaller space with just a few tables, and he closes the door behind us. We are alone.

Ryker's high cheekbones should be ruddy as they usually are when he gets off the mountain, especially on a windy day like today. But they are pale, and I know I'm already freaking him out, even though I haven't said a word. I suppose this isn't like me, not at all.

"Relax, Ryker, okay?" My immediate instinct is to soothe him, but I brought this on for a reason, and the conversation needs to happen. "Have you realized yet that we are basically going to be separated for the next six months?"

Ryker's expression morphs from anxious to questioning. "What? Why?"

"First I go to Europe, then you'll be traveling for business, and then summer."

"Wait, I never talked to you about business. I'll have to travel when the season is done, but I won't be gone all the time." Even as he says it, I can see the realization sinking in for him as well.

"Player mentioned that you'll have to travel a lot as soon as snowboarding competitions wrap up."

He lets out a frustrated sigh. "It's true, but it's not like I'll never be here. And summer, well, we can still see each other."

I'm not ready to think about Ryker visiting Vermont and how weird that would be, and it's not like I'll be able to fly around the country to see him over the summer. I want to take it all back. It's ridiculous that we've been a couple only a few days and I'm forcing this conversation. But it seems like it has to happen. This doesn't feel like the kind of relationship that can just go with the flow.

Ryker runs a hand over his face. "Look, Roxanne, I'm already seeing things differently, okay? I wanted to figure it out on my own before speaking with you, or anyone, about it, but I don't want you to worry so much."

"What are you saying, Ryker?"

"I'm stepping down as CEO of Stark, Inc."

I suck in a breath and step backward, without even meaning to.

He doesn't notice my reaction. "It's not going to happen overnight or even in the next few weeks. It'll take some time. But this is something that needs to happen, and meeting you helped me realize that."

I'm shaking my head, trying hard not to gasp for breath. I don't want him to know that the air in the room suddenly feels thick like syrup. It's clogging my lungs.

"When I started acting as CEO from behind the computer, years ago, I didn't really think about the consequences. At least, not in the way I do now. I'm living in two different worlds, and even if I'm balancing it, it's not sustainable. I could pull it off until I graduate, but then what? I'm halfway into both of them, and I have to pick. Meeting you helped me see that. Being with you helped me realize which one I want to choose."

"Ryker, no. You can't," I struggle to say. "You can't just get out of your family business like that. And you're so good at it. You can't walk away." Not because of *me*.

Ryker was leaning forward, reaching to me, pleading for me to understand, and now he shifts back, upright, putting distance between us. Just as I have.

"You should know, Roxanne, that I don't respond well to commands." Whoa, scary Ryker is back. And he's got that business voice on. "And it's not a family business anymore. Not really. My mother alienated my relatives. A few have even sold their shares. They're distant cousins, some of whom I've never even met."

A surge of sadness wraps around me. It sounds so very lonely. "Why did you do it? Why do you put so much into it? You must care." My voice is just above a whisper, as if my questions could set him off if asked with too much force.

He shrugs and looks away. "Those are complicated questions." He's not going to respond to them, and even as we stand there, a few feet apart, emotions swirling between us, I know I've put him on the spot. This wasn't supposed to turn into a therapy session, and maybe I'm not being fair.

He keeps talking, but veers in another direction. "I will always be involved in Stark, Inc. to some degree, and I'll probably continue to hold a certain level of leadership in the winter sports community, if unofficial. But I want to be a real student at Stark."

That makes me smile, and he huffs out a little laugh, recognizing that he'll never be a normal student, not really. "Well, I at least need to scale back my responsibilities." There's so much more to that statement, I know there is. I want to ask him how snowboarding makes him feel. Is that when he gets to be carefree? Does his role as business leader give him a sense of worth he never felt from his ice queen of a mother? Is he willing to give that up in order to have a sense of normalcy?

I wonder if he thinks of himself as superhuman and invincible, because I know that, even when I despised him, I couldn't help but wonder if he had superpowers. Is he shedding that image because it's become too burdensome? I watched him at the party on Thanksgiving and I saw him just this morning in his office. It didn't seem like Ryker the CEO took any extra energy from him. Or maybe Ryker is just really good at hiding weakness.

Ryker's face suddenly softens and he steps forward, wrapping his arms around my waist. "This doesn't change anything between us, okay? All it means is that, at some point in the near future, I'll be more present when I'm with you. And I'll have more time. I'll be fully in this world, with you. It doesn't mean I expect anything from you."

I didn't even realize that's what I was fearing until he said it and soothed it away. Well, not totally, but mostly.

"There isn't going to be a hole you have to fill in my life, or anything like that. All I meant to say was that you helped me make a decision that I needed to make anyway. Without you, I might have dropped out of school, gotten more wrapped up in the business and stopped competing at snowboarding. I would have felt like I was sixty years old by the time I turned twenty-one. And if I keep trying to do it all I'll go crazy or burn out in an epic fire. I know it. I've seen it happen to people. The business side and the athlete side. People get greedy and mess it all up. This is the right choice, and I needed a reason to make it. You're that reason. That's all."

# Chapter 6

The things Ryker has told me in the past ten minutes are more than he's ever revealed about who he is and who he wants to be, even in the six months I've known him. I feel as if he's opening a door for me, one he's never shown anyone else, and asking me to walk inside with him. I jump.

My arms wrap around his neck and I try to tell him with my body that yes, I'm happy to be his reason for choosing this. I won't second-guess his decision, and I'll try not to fear what it means for me, or for us. Whatever is happening between us is moving at lightning speed now. In a way, it came suddenly and unexpectedly, the two of us together. But on the other hand, it seemed inevitable; it was just a matter of us getting on the same page, or being willing to get on the same page.

Only last week, I wouldn't have believed it if someone told me I'd be in a private dining room kissing Ryker, losing all sense of reality as my legs wound around his waist and he pushed me back against a wall. Ryker's confident in his decision, and he only wants me to be cool with it, not worry or make it a big deal. He's not asking for my approval or even for my opinion. And he shouldn't have to. It's just us here, together, bodies molding against the wall, and the rest of the world will fall into place around us. It has to.

"Uh, guys?" The sound of Player's voice breaks us apart. Neither of us even heard the door open. My body slowly slides down the wall and Ryker's hand slips away from underneath my shirt. Ryker's body is hard against mine, and it shields me from Player. Of all people to walk in on us, Player is probably the least embarrassing, but my cheeks still flame. The moment was so intense and intimate, it feels wrong for anyone else to step into it.

Ryker must be giving Player a death glare because he looks a little nervous when he explains, "The teachers just started showing up for a meeting. They're getting food now but should be in here any minute."

"Thanks," Ryker and I say in unison. Yeah, that would have been even more embarrassing.

Player's unable to hide his grin as he shakes his head and backs out the door. We take a minute to straighten ourselves out before following behind him. In the hallway, Ryker takes my hand. "We're good, right?"

I nod. "We're good."

Ryker's stepping down as CEO of Stark, Inc. sometime soon and I might be the only person who knows it. The depth of his trust in me is more shocking than the decision itself. I'm not even sure how I earned it, or when it happened. Ryker's not holding back in this relationship, not one bit, and it scares me. I don't know if I'm ready for something so serious. I'm only seventeen years old.

Ryker tells me he's going to grab some food, and I take the opportunity to head out. I've already eaten enough and I need a moment alone. How did this all happen so fast? And am I okay with it?

I've never even wanted a relationship before, and actually, I've always avoided them. Chelsea Radner, my best girlfriend back in Ashfield, Vermont, and her boyfriend, Tyler Luck, are the only people I know who have pulled off a relationship in high school that seems worthwhile. I've watched so many others get wrapped up in each other and fall apart, wanting so badly to be in love that they trick even themselves or try to force it when it's not there. And I've always had so much going on without that kind of distraction. Skiing is my love, and that's more than enough. My relationships are friendships, not romantic ones, even if one of my best friends since kindergarten, Brad Samuel, wants more with me. He hasn't outright said so, not exactly, but I'm pretty sure if I made a move, it'd happen between us.

I find myself calling Chelsea, needing to talk to someone who isn't wrapped up in the Stark world. She answers on the first ring.

"Roxie girl!"

"Hi, Chelsea, whatcha doin'?" I want to make sure she's alone before I start pouring out my soul.

"On my way to the gym for a lifting session. You know Sugarville is freaking out about you, right? People won't stop talking about what you did at the Beaver Creek Carnival." She starts telling me about people I hardly know who now talk about me as if we are close friends. "I think when you come back, you'll be like a celebrity."

I never told anyone about my plan to finish out this year at Stark, prove myself to the posse, and then return home for my senior year. And I'm glad I didn't, because everything has changed these past few days, and I plan on being at Stark again next year.

"Yeah, that's going to be weird." A celebrity in my hometown? I doubt it will still be like that by this summer. People will get over it.

"So, how's the hunky boyfriend?" she asks.

"Hunky? Really, Chels? You sound like my mother." I ignore the boyfriend part, which still weirds me out.

"Aw, cute! You told your mom about him."

"She saw him kiss me on national television, remember?" Yeah, everyone knew about it before I'd even really had time to let it sink in myself.

"That was sweet," she says dreamily, and then she perks up, remembering something. "So, I've got pretty epic news."

"Oh yeah?"

"Our updated FIS rankings came through yesterday, and the coaches got together to decide on the competition schedule. We're going to be at the same races as you!"

"What?!" I knew they'd all had great races over the weekend, but I had no idea they were all so close to moving up a level.

"Tyler had already qualified, actually, but the little shit didn't tell me. Only Dani Frye and her boyfriend Wyatt Jenkins," she starts to explain but I interrupt her.

"Dani and Wyatt are together? Since when?" They're both really strong racers but probably two of the quietest people I've ever met.

"Who knows? Before Christmas. You know it's like pulling teeth to get info from those two. Anyway, they were the only ones who had made the Sugarville A team this year, and Tyler figured he'd come with me and Brad on the B team. But now we're all coming!"

"This is awesome! Now I don't have to be so nervous about racing the more competitive FIS races. I'm so glad you guys will be there for my first trip to Europe. I mean, if you idiots are going to be there, it's not so scary." My friends have gone in past years, racing at the lower level FIS races, but it was never in the budget for my family.

FIS stands for Federation International du Ski, and points are equivalent to rankings; the lower, the better. You get a score in each discipline, and then a combined one for all four: slalom, giant slalom (GS), Super-G, and downhill. The FIS races we're going to in Europe are the most competitive ones before the Europa Cup, which is the highest level before World Cup races. It'll be my first time even racing in Europe, and I'm only able to afford it because I have a full scholarship to Stark, which includes travel to competitions.

"I'll email you our schedule and where we're staying and stuff."

We spend the next twenty minutes talking about the races we'll be at together. The first stop is France, then Austria, and then Italy. We have to get off when she gets to the gym and I get to my first class but I'm reeling with the news that my closest friends will be with me over there. I know I won't be able to spend every minute with them and that we'll be super busy racing and training, but it's still comforting knowing they will be on the same mountains at the same time. I didn't realize I'd been harboring some anxiety about the trip until it released with Chelsea's news.

Brad calls between classes later to tell me the same news, and he's ecstatic, mostly because it's a huge deal to qualify for these races.

Well, I hope that's the main reason for his enthusiasm, but I know he's missing me, and not in the same way I miss him. The distance has somehow made it clearer for me to see Brad's feelings toward me. It's like his true emotions are no longer clouded and obscured by our everyday routines and the mundane parts of our days that we used to share together.

Brad knows about Ryker, of course. He saw the kiss on TV, like everyone else. Ryker knew the cameras were there at the half-pipe competition, following him, and he was making a statement. When I spoke with Brad on the phone the next day, he only said, "So, you and Ryker Black, huh?" and I said, "Yeah," and that was that. We didn't get into it.

I know Brad probably had to hold himself back from telling me why it's a bad idea to be with Ryker. He knows that if he goes there, he's getting into dangerous territory, where his own motives for not wanting me in a relationship could come into play. Ingrid and Monica can warn me away, but Brad might come off as jealous. I don't think either Brad or I want to put our friendship to the test like that. If there's one thing I've learned being friends with Brad for so long, it's that some things are better left unsaid.

*** 

Ryker catches me leaving the gym later that afternoon, and he asks me why I look so happy. Oh. He reads me better than anyone else, I think. One of his many skills, I suppose. But I hesitate before telling him, and then, for reasons I'll have to think about later, I lie. Or omit the truth.

"It might be from this amazing make-out session I had at DH earlier. The guy was really hot. Great body." I'm flirting to distract him, and the guilt flares. We've dealt with so much in the few days since we've gotten together as a couple, and I just can't handle another curveball right now. I hadn't thought about it until he asked, but Brad Samuel being in the same place as me for three weeks, without Ryker, will definitely cause some issues. I mean, Ryker didn't even like the idea of Brad being around me when my friends came out to visit over Thanksgiving. And Ryker and I were more like make-out frenemies or something back then. Definitely not a couple.

The flirting distracts Ryker. "I hope you like this guy, because he wants to take you home with him."

*Home with him.* That sounds awesome.

"Can we swing by my dorm so I can pack a bag this time?"

"Sure. Pack one for the rest of the week."

I had said one night at a time before, but there's no point in arguing now. We should spend as much time together as we can. Because after this week, who knows?

The atmosphere is totally different from last night when we step into his house. It's like a match was lit at DH earlier, and the heat level between us is on full blast. We'd talked about dinner, but all thoughts of eating disappear when our lips collide in the mudroom. We don't even make it all the way inside.

Ryker tugs off his jacket and my own as we keep our lips locked. He must really like holding me up against walls because he has me up against one again as soon as our shoes are kicked off. My legs wrap around his waist, and my hands slide under his shirt, holding on to his shoulders.

When he starts to tug my shirt off, I hesitate for an instant, having never gone this far before, but then it's over my head and he's taking me in, looking at me like he's never seen breasts before and he's totally fascinated. I know this isn't a first for him, even without the gossip mill telling me so. No, he touches me and moves with enough confidence to convey that he's got plenty of experience with a woman's body.

But he's gentle with me when he reaches for my chest, moving slowly, and it makes me wonder if he knows I've never let a guy see me half-naked like this. I'm nervous. I don't even know why. I guess

I feel so exposed, like I'm giving him something, offering a precious part of me, and what he does with it is very important to me.

Ryker leans down to kiss every inch of my torso, cherishing it, and I know he understands. He's not taking it lightly. No, his kisses along my skin are meaningful ones. Even if he's done it before, I know he's taking his time because it matters to him just like it matters to me. We aren't just bodies to each other.

"Upstairs?" he asks quietly. He's taken control and slowed the pace, though both of us are breathing heavily.

I don't want to stop. I really don't want to stop. But I know that I should. My body is ready for the next step; hell, it's ready to run up the entire staircase, figuratively and literally, I guess, but the rest of me, my head and my heart, want to slow down.

I feel so stupid saying it, and I'm worried how he'll react, since he's clearly pretty worked up here, but I do it anyway.

"I think we should take a breather. Eat something. Cool off." My voice shakes a little, mostly because I'm still super turned on and it would take very little convincing for me to jump on him again.

But Ryker surprises me when he nods in agreement. For a guy who usually gets right down to business with girls, he doesn't seem at all disappointed with slowing it down. Actually, he looks a little relieved. Which is weird.

"That's okay?" I ask.

He puts his hands on the counter, getting ahold of himself, and I slide my shirt back on. "Yeah, of course it's okay, Roxanne. I'm glad you spoke up, because I got caught up in the moment. I don't want to move too fast with you, and I would've had trouble putting on the brakes on my own."

"Oh." Does he know how inexperienced I am? Is that why he doesn't want to move too fast with me? Should I tell him I've never done much more than kiss? Not right now. We need to think about something else.

"So, dinner?" He pushes off the counter and opens the fridge.

"Yeah," I say, breathing out heavily. "Dinner."

# Chapter 7

The routine that develops over the next few days would freak me out if I wasn't leaving for Europe. Each morning I wake up in Ryker's bed, get coffee in his kitchen, and find him in the study. We eat breakfast together before going to the mountain to train with our teams. Then we go to DH together to eat a second breakfast, unless one of us has to go straight to class. We usually meet again for lunch at DH, depending on class schedule, and then we each go to the gym to work out in the afternoon. We've gotten in the habit of going straight to Ryker's house after the gym, where we kiss a little, eat, and Ryker goes to the study to do some work while I shower and call my parents. We kiss some more before going to sleep next to each other.

Basically, we spend every spare minute together. I used to think couples like us were disillusioned, chasing after a void in their lives or just super horny or something. And I guess I do feel a little bit dizzy, like I'm under a spell, at times, but I know it's going to come to a halt when I get on the plane, and that makes me willing to just go with it for now, and not worry about what it means.

It's Sunday, and the Europe team leaves tomorrow. There are ten of us, five girls and five guys, on Stark's A team. It's only considered the "A" team for this trip, because another group is also going to Europe, but to less competitive races. Probably the same ones my Vermont friends were originally going to race.

Petra and Ingrid are on the girls' A team, of course, and Sven on the guys' team. Petra's been lying low since she showed up at Ryker's last week, and I only hope she stays out of my way on the trip. She's a serious skier, and I'd be surprised if she let herself get distracted from the races because of some plot to annoy me. That's what I'm banking on, at least.

In addition to me, Petra and Ingrid, the other two girls on the trip are Sofia Bassino and Sydney Patzer. Sofia's a junior from a tiny town in the Dolomites in Italy, and Sydney's a senior from Park

City, Utah. The two of them are best friends, as far as I can tell, and I'm not sure what Sofia's going to do when Sydney graduates this year. Sydney's got a spot on a few college teams but I think she's hoping to earn a spot on the National Team instead. Both girls are nice enough, but they never reached out to be my friend. At least, not like Ingrid did that first day.

On the guys' team, the brothers Jasper and Dominic Rhodes, a sophomore and a senior, are from Breckenridge, Colorado, I think. I'm pretty sure Dominic, the senior, already has a spot on the U.S. National Team, it's just a matter of whether he'll be on A, B, C, or D team next year. Chad Robbins is a junior like me, and he's from Truckee, California. Henrik is also a junior and has, like, an eight-syllable last name that I have no idea how to pronounce. Henrik's dad is Norwegian and his mom is from Vail, Colorado.

I really like Henrik, and we've chatted a few times on chair lift rides. He's ski royalty, with parents who both raced on their National Teams, and a father who went to the Olympics in Giant Slalom. He was born in Norway but went back and forth a lot until starting Stark in the seventh grade. His parents visit frequently, and his little sister is a freshman on the team. I think Henrik would probably be in the posse next year, if it still existed. He might have been on it this year, actually, if Sven hadn't been the representative from the guys' ski team. Actually, I have no idea if it works that way, and Ryker did invite me when he already had a girl skier in the group. And Ryker and Player are both snowboarders, but Ryker doesn't totally count like a normal person. Ugh. Who knows, who cares?

I still haven't told Ryker about my Vermont friends being at the same races. I don't want to break this spell, or whatever it is, between us. Things are good. Really good. But I know he'll find out eventually, and with less than twenty-four hours to go, I'd rather do it here in person than over the phone.

Our last night together, we're not alone. Ryker invites the rest of our friends over to his place, and this time I invite Monica, Liam and Misha. Over the past week, there's definitely been some confusion amongst Stark students about what's going on with the posse. We keep repeating that there isn't one anymore, but people continue trying to define a new one, watching who Ryker interacts with, who he sits with, who he seems to ignore or give special treatment to. It'd be sort of comical if it wasn't so aggravating.

At least Monica and my other friends seem to understand that things have changed, and we don't have to label who matters like we used to. There's still power at the top, that will never change, but it's a different kind of power, and, well, some of it is in my hands.

I almost invite some others on our team, just to prevent the appearance that a new "posse" is forming, but really, the people here tonight are my closest friends, and if I invite a couple more, then I'll feel like I have to invite everyone so as not to be exclusive, and then it will just turn into a giant party, which isn't really what I'm in the mood for. Ugh. I don't want to overanalyze it, and being in this position of supposed authority makes me feel obligated to get it right before I screw it all up. It's probably a good thing I'm leaving tomorrow for three weeks.

We're upstairs in Ryker's loft, enjoying all the toys – foosball, pool, table tennis, and air hockey – when Sven drops the bomb I've been carrying around all week.

We're playing air hockey against each other when he says, "How awesome is it that your Vermont friends are going to be at the same FIS races as us?"

Ryker is standing right behind him, facing the other way as he plays foosball against Cody, and his shoulders stiffen, telling me he heard the question.

"Oh, uh, yeah, I just found that out. How did you know?"

"Oh, I'm Facebook friends with all of them. Saw some posts about it on Brad's page. He's a cool guy. Hopefully we'll all get a chance to hang out."

I can't tear my eyes away from the back of Ryker's head. He's still playing foosball, but the way he turns the handles, almost violently, says that this news is pissing him off. I knew I should have just told him earlier.

"Yeah. I'm sure we'll be really busy so we might not have much time to chill. Chelsea's been to Europe the past two years for FIS races, and she said they barely saw anything except the mountain and the hotel rooms because all they did was train, race, and sleep."

"Can't forget eating," Ingrid calls out from her ping pong match against Telluride. "I had fondue every night we were in Switzerland last year."

"We aren't going to Switzerland this year," I remind her. "Just flying into Geneva, but we'll only be there for like, a minute. Do they have fondue in France?" The conversation shifts to cuisine, and I'm grateful.

But as the night goes on, Ryker won't look at me. I try to stand beside him so I can say something or touch him in reassurance, but he ignores me. It's like all those months when he ignored me on campus, and it reopens barely-healed wounds. It hurts, and it makes me angry.

He doesn't really have a right to react like this, does he? What's the big deal? I could've found out earlier today, for all he knows. Except, he knows that I talk to my friends from Vermont almost every day, and that there's no way they only found out about this today. The most recent FIS list came in a week ago, and that's when people would've found out which races they were going to.

Ryker's too plugged into the ski world to be fooled. My friends have known for a week now, which means I have too. And I haven't told him. And he knows why. Yeah, this isn't good.

I'm aware of the clock ticking all night long, and no one seems eager to leave. The ski team, at least, doesn't have practice in the morning. We get to "sleep in" until seven and then we cram in extra classes before we leave for the airport in the afternoon. The first leg of the flight is from Stark to Chicago, and then we have a layover before boarding a red-eye flight to Geneva. It's the closest major airport to Chamonix, France, where the first set of races takes place.

I'm distracted when the snowboarders, hockey players and figure skaters hug us goodbye, but I guess the hugs are meant more for encouragement and well-wishes than goodbyes. We're only leaving for three weeks, but it's an important three weeks. We'll be competing against some of the best ski racers in the world. The snowboarders will be leaving for their own tour around North America in a couple of days, and it's kind of up to the skaters – hockey and figure skating both – to hold down the fort. I don't even know what that means, besides keeping things rolling in the same direction. No more rules. So yeah, less work for them, right? No one to keep in check or whatever it is the posse used to do.

It's almost midnight when Ryker and I are finally alone.

We're standing in the loft by the railing, having just waved to Player and Telly in the front foyer. When the door shuts behind them, I tense. Will he storm off? Was he just waiting for everyone to leave before he let loose on me? I know that Ryker isn't used to being messed with, and I wonder if that's what he thinks I'm doing. *Is* it what I'm doing? Why was I so afraid to tell him? Why did I wait?

I don't even remember anymore.

He stands very still when I turn to him, but he's not ignoring me now. Ryker's looking at me like he wants to figure me out. Like I'm a puzzle to solve, and it brings me back to that first day he walked into my dorm room. The turquoise eyes pulled me in then and they're doing it now.

"I'm sorry I didn't tell you about my Vermont friends racing the same FIS circuit as us." I mean it, and I hope he knows I'm sincere.

Ryker's hard expression softens for an instant, and I see the hurt there before he covers it up again, tightening his jaw and wiping his face clean of any sign of vulnerability. It's enough though. It tells me that he wasn't ignoring me all night as a power play, or a punishment. No, he ignored me because my lack of honesty felt like a betrayal, and he was hurt.

He swallows hard before asking, "Why didn't you say anything?" I think it takes effort on his part to ask the question without revealing how deep it cut him.

It's a little thing, in some ways. But it's a big thing, too.

"I was going to," I start to say, and his eyes flash, like he doesn't believe me. Maybe he's right. "I remembered how you were about Brad at Thanksgiving," I finally admit. I get right to the heart of the matter. "Things have been so good with us this week, and with everything else going on with the princesses and Stark, Inc., I didn't want to upset you."

"Upset me?" Ryker sounds amused, but there's a dark note behind it, too.

"I thought you might pull away, or, I don't know. I knew you wouldn't like it."

"You should have told me, Roxanne," he says sternly, and I feel like I'm being scolded. But as he continues, the tough act crumbles away and he shows me why this hit him so hard. "I've opened up to you in ways I've never opened up to anyone. About my family, my work, my life. It might not seem like much, but I've let you in further than anyone else. Sometimes it comes naturally, but sometimes it's hard, because I don't know how you'll react or if you'll like it."

He's lecturing me, I guess, but it also feels like he's pouring his heart out. Letting it bleed right here on the carpet.

Ryker steps forward. We're not touching, but we're breathing the same air. He lowers his voice. "You've been open too, I think. But when you hide something from me because you think it will upset me, well, it makes me wonder what else you hide. I don't want that between us."

"I'm not hiding anything from you, Ryker," I assure him.

"I hope not." He says it like a plea, when it could be a threat.

My hand reaches up to his cheek, and he captures it before I can touch him. Ryker pulls me into a deep kiss that I'm unprepared for. It's not filled with lust, not exactly, but there's a passion there that's heavy with emotion. I have the power to hurt Ryker Black, and that scares me. It feels like I'm an unwilling kryptonite to his Superman. But am I good for him, too?

When we climb in bed that night, Ryker spoons his body around mine, running his hands up and down my stomach.

"I'm going to miss you, Ryker," I tell the dark room.

He hums into the back of my head. "I always miss you, Roxanne. Remember that."

I'm exhausted and it's well past my bedtime, but it takes me hours to fall asleep. I'm thinking about kryptonite and superheroes, and how Ryker Black is a prodigy in more ways than one. He's going to leave his position as a leader of his family business, and he says I "helped" him make that decision. It's not up to me to question that, to wonder if it's what's best for him, except here I am, curled up in his bed. Am I weakening this powerful and talented guy? Or am I strengthening him? Is it possible to do both? I don't want to hurt him again, I know that much. I only hope it's within my control.

# Chapter 8

I'm in Switzerland. *Switzerland*. It's late morning here, but it feels like the middle of the night to me. Lia and Rocco warned us to put in earplugs and sleep as soon as they finished the dinner service but... well, there were some really good movies playing for free and the next thing I knew, we were touching down in Geneva. We're waiting by the baggage carousel, and the rush of adrenaline at being in a foreign country is wearing off fast. I'm dizzy with fatigue, and suffering a major headache.

I might even fall asleep standing up.

"Drink this." Ingrid shoves a plastic cup of hot coffee in front of me, and even though I feel a little queasy after sitting on a plane for eight hours, I know that I won't make it to the mountain if I don't get some caffeine in my veins.

Ingrid explains how to order coffee around here, but I don't process much. People around us are speaking French or German, making my foggy brain even more confused.

"You're a mess, Roxie," Sven says. "You can sleep on the van ride to Chamonix. It's a two-hour drive. But we're hitting the slopes this afternoon, so you're going to have to power on through."

I'm in Europe for the first time, and the idea of snapping into skis makes me feel slightly ill. Yeah, two nights in a row without much sleep has caught up to me. Ugh.

"Is that your phone beeping, Ingrid?" I ask. Someone keeps sending her text messages.

"Yes, it's my annoying brother. Tabor. He's coming to watch us race and he won't stop texting me about it."

"I didn't even know you had a brother. How old is he?"

"Fourteen," she says with a sigh.

"Why isn't he at Stark, then?"

"Oh, he's not good enough. I mean, he's good, but not good enough for Stark." Wow. The Koller family is pretty well-known in the alpine skiing world, and Ingrid is already a Stark student, yet her younger brother isn't Stark caliber. If that's not a reminder of how lucky I am to be here, I don't know what is. I have to wonder if that's why she never mentioned him before.

"Roxie Slade!" The high-pitched voice cuts through my aching brain, but still, it makes me smile.

Chelsea Radner is jogging my way, wearing sweatpants and a Sugarville hoodie, looking like she just rolled out of bed. When she reaches me, she wraps me in a hug, and I think she must transfer some of her energy to me, because I instantly feel a little spark. When Tyler embraces me a moment later, I feel even more invigorated.

"Wait, I thought you guys got in a few hours ago? Why are you still at the airport?" I ask, confused.

"Flight was delayed off the ground," Tyler explains. "We just landed."

"Where's Brad?" I ask, looking around.

"Getting coffee. He never sleeps on the plane ride over." Tyler shakes his head. "Every year the idiot watches movies instead of sleeping and suffers the next day."

Chelsea rolls her eyes. "Yup, he'll be moaning and groaning for the rest of the day. I should've slipped some Ambien in his drink. Darn. There's always next year."

Ingrid laughs. "Yeah, our girl here did the same thing. Stayed up the entire flight."

I nod and sigh at my stupidity. I do feel better now, and as a few other Sugarville skiers and coaches notice us and trickle over to say hello, I find myself surrounded by my new team and my old one. Petra keeps her distance until Brad shows up, and then it's like she can't help herself. A hot skier who races in her league is Petra

Hoffman's ideal target, at least now that Ryker isn't an option. She knows he's my good friend, but she doesn't know that I never told him what she did to me. No, I never told any of my Vermont friends about that night. They'd freak and tell me to come home.

But what if I had? As soon as Brad releases me from a long hug, Petra's on him, acting like they're all buddy-buddy from the time we spent hanging out over Thanksgiving break. I have the strange urge to growl at her to back off. It's not that I'm jealous, but I am protective of Brad. At home in Vermont, I never really needed to vet the girls who wanted him, but I know that Petra is bad news. She could do some serious damage, depending on what her goal is here. It hadn't even occurred to me until just now that she would use him to hurt me.

Brad's wary though, because he at least knows she's been bitchy to me, even if he isn't clued in on the entire extent of it. And he's seriously jet-lagged like me. He tries to brush her off, but it's not until I step forcefully between then, effectively pushing her out of the way, that she backs off.

"I heard you stayed up the entire flight. Join the club," I tell him.

He smiles sheepishly. "I should know better. I just hate sleeping on planes. It depresses me."

I laugh at that remark. And then I feel guilty. I'm leaning into Brad's chest, taking comfort in his familiarity, and I *know* how he feels about me, and how Ryker feels about Brad getting too close to me. I'm almost too tired to care. It'd be nice to fall asleep standing up right here, resting my head on his chest. Besides, Ryker had already left when I woke up this morning. The coffee pot was full, but there was no note, and he wasn't in the study like he usually is. I thought I'd catch him around campus before we left but I never saw him.

It's only three weeks.

Is it stupid that I miss him already? Yeah, definitely. I probably just need a nap.

We split with the Sugarville team as we each collect our luggage and find the shuttle vans taking us to Chamonix, where we'll stay for the first week. We'll run into each other again soon. I know I should take in the scenery, but there's no fighting my heavy eyelids – as soon as the van starts moving, I'm out.

The nap is enough to get me through the first training afternoon, but I'm basically half asleep as I run through the gates. We're training slalom, my worst discipline, but Lia lays off for this once, and I'm grateful for the reprieve. As soon as we're off the mountain, I call my parents to let them know I arrived safely. They upgraded to an international phone plan for our cell phones this month.

I grab a sandwich at a café for dinner, thankful that most people speak English, since the resort is a tourist destination. I'm sharing a room with Ingrid, and as soon as I've showered, my head hits the pillow. The lights are all on, since Ingrid is still up, unpacking her things, but I don't care. It's not until I start to drift to sleep that I realize I never heard from Ryker.

Even though my hours are all screwed up, I sleep straight through for nearly twelve hours, waking just before six AM. My body is still confused about what's going on, but I feel so much better. The first thing I do is check my phone. Texts from Brad and Chelsea after I crashed last night, asking if I want to grab dinner, but nothing from Ryker.

I'd only sent him one text after we arrived, letting him know we made it, and it's weird he wouldn't get back to me with at least a short reply. We hadn't discussed how often we'd talk, or not talk, while I was in Europe, but I figured there'd be at least some communication.

I bundle up to head outside and look for breakfast, leaving Ingrid sleeping in our room. Colorado is eight hours behind France, so it's almost 10 PM there. Even though we went to bed a little before that when I slept over with Ryker, there's a chance he might stay up later when I'm not around.

Ryker answers on the first ring, and hearing his voice makes me way too happy.

"Roxanne."

"Hey."

"You're up early."

"Yeah, my body's confused. But we're meeting in two hours to run gates anyway, so I figured I'd scope out the town."

"You're outside?"

"Yeah, it's freezing."

Ryker laughs quietly, and though it's nice to hear, I'd prefer him at my side. I'm a little repulsed by my own thoughts. Since when did I become such a sap?

"How was the flight and your first day in Europe?"

"A daze." I tell him about how I didn't sleep and was a basket case yesterday. I want to ask why he never called or returned my text, but I don't want to sound like a clingy girlfriend. Am I a clingy girlfriend? I shudder at the idea, not from the cold.

"Your teeth are chattering, Roxanne." Ryker hears my shaky breathing from the other end of the phone, but he doesn't realize it's because I'm freaking out about my attachment to him. "Go inside."

"I just passed a place that smelled amazing. But it doesn't look like they have one-stop shops. Do bread places sell coffee?"

"Sometimes."

"I hope they speak English."

"Just point and smile. You'll do great."

"Thanks for the vote of confidence." I feel stupid telling a guy like Ryker that I'm nervous ordering breakfast in a foreign country. My lack of worldly experience, not to mention other kinds of experience, is way more apparent next to a guy like him.

"I'll call when it's my morning, okay?"

My chest surges happily at his promise, which then makes my stomach turn, troubled by my reaction. Man, my body really is confused, and not just from the time change.

"Sounds good. Night, Ryker."

"Morning, Roxanne. Have a good training session."

The man in the *boulangerie* is friendly and he speaks enough broken English to make for a smooth transaction. I get a few different things, since it all looks delicious, and I'm sure Ingrid can help me with whatever I can't finish.

When the little old man points to the emblem on my jacket and asks, "You from Stark?" with a heavy accent, I'm reminded again that my team, my school, is known all over the world, even by a guy at a bread shop in Chamonix, France.

Knowing I'm representing Stark brings me pride I haven't experienced before, and I wonder if it's because I have a newfound respect and understanding of the boy behind it. Yes, there's a line of Starks who came before him, but he's at the heart of the school.

When I turn the corner to our hotel, I see Chelsea and Tyler walking down the nearly empty street hand in hand. The sight makes me smile. They are so good together. But it also comes with a new sensation, a little wistfulness, I guess.

They spot me and wave.

"Is that food you have in the bag?" Chelsea asks.

"Maybe."

"Don't mess with the girl, Roxie. She woke up starving. I thought she was going to eat my arm off."

"You guys sharing a room?"

Tyler nods. "Unofficially, yeah." He starts to explain how Chelsea's roommate, Dani Frye, is sleeping in her boyfriend Wyatt's room, because he doesn't have a roommate, while Tyler stays in Chelsea's room. Chelsea gets impatient with the explanation and snatches the bag out of my hands.

"Is this a chocolate croissant?" she asks, eyeing the first thing she pulls out of the bag.

"I believe it's called *pain chocolat.*"

She takes a huge mouthful. "*Pain au chocolat,*" she corrects me through a mouthful of dough.

"You picked a real polite one, Ty. Stealing food off an innocent girl on the street. I overcame some serious anxiety to order that pastry, Chels."

She's not buying it. "Puh-lease. You have enough to feed an army in that bag. Or, like, three skiers. Whichever."

Chelsea and Tyler point out their hotel to me, which is right across the street from mine. We're at the base of the mountain, the ski lifts only steps away, and even though the streets are wide enough for cars, I've barely seen any pass through. The village is basically giant pedestrian sidewalks filled with hotels, cafés, restaurants, bars, and ski shops. It's ideal for what we're here to do.

Tyler and Chelsea head off to load up on their own stock of croissants and I head into the hotel lobby, where I'm grateful to find coffee available. With caffeine, food and a good night's rest, I'm finally ready to make some turns on a French ski slope. I know I did it yesterday, but I don't think that counts, since I was hardly coherent. I wonder if the snow will feel different. Maybe my skis will know it's European snow. French snow. Yeah, I need coffee.

"Someone looks like they came back to life," Lia Moretti tells me from her spot at a small table in the breakfast area. "You know, you don't need to leave for breakfast. They start serving it here at six each morning."

I shrug. "I was up before then, and I wanted to check out the village." I take a seat beside her, since there's no one else around. "Sorry I was so out of it yesterday. I'll be sharper today."

Lia nods. "Good. It's Wednesday and there's not much time to adjust. We train GS today, slalom tomorrow. You race slalom Friday and giant slalom Sunday."

I take a sip of coffee and ask when the lifts start running.

"Eight. That's when we meet in the lobby and walk over together. You should have the schedule." Lia isn't mean, just straight to the point. There's no space for sloppiness in her world.

"Yeah, I know when we're meeting. I'm just excited. I was looking at the slopes this morning and they're freshly groomed. Looks like they got a couple inches last night. Yesterday was such a fog that I'm eager for a redo."

Lia's lips lift in a tight smile, but not a forced one. She's just not the type to be all exuberant about anything. "Want to do a couple runs before we set up gates?" she asks mischievously.

"I thought the lifts didn't open until eight?"

"I've got connections." She actually waggles her eyebrows, I think. Whoa. Maybe Lia isn't as uptight as I thought.

"Then yeah, definitely. Let's go."

Lia and Rocco gave us a very strict schedule, which doesn't involve any free skiing, aside from warm-up runs. Free skiing is what most people do when they ski – go down slopes without thinking about much of anything except having fun. For us, almost every run down the mountain involves running through the gates, or setting up the course or taking it down. It's a special treat to break the rules and get some fun runs in first thing in the morning.

Ingrid is still asleep and I change quickly, meeting Lia by the ski lockers in back of the hotel, where we unload our skis and walk over to the lift. When she walks into the operator's office, unlocking it with a key in her hand, it flashes me back to that first night I skied at Stark, before the mountain was officially open for the season. Ryker started the lift that night, and we rode up together while everyone else was still asleep.

Breaking into the chair lift control rooms must be a Stark Springs Academy thing, because Lia comes out a moment later just as the lift starts roaring to life. She's smiling widely this time, and I know this is another special moment I'll keep in my memories. Hard-ass Lia Moretti beaming from a little rule-breaking. I guess everyone needs to break rules now and then.

# Chapter 9

After that first morning skiing with Lia, the trip gets back on the right foot. I'm filled with energy and determination on the training days, and we have more time to rest than usual. We actually have naps scheduled into our day each afternoon, in place of our typical gym workout. Or at least, "down time" in our rooms. We're also supposed to be doing some class work, but it's no more than an hour each day, after naptime and before dinner. Aside from breakfast at the hotel, we're free to do what we want for meals, and my stipend covers that expense as well.

Ingrid, Sven and I usually eat lunches and dinners with Brad, Tyler and Chelsea. Sometimes the others on the Stark team join us, and Dani and Wyatt ate lunch with us one time. Petra must be flying solo. Two weeks ago, the others on our team would have been thrilled to have Petra join them, but she's become a pariah amongst Stark students, and no one wants to associate with her.

Ryker and I have talked on the phone a couple more times, but it's mostly by text. It's too tricky trying to connect with the different time zones, and he left on Thursday for a competition in Vancouver, making it even harder to get in touch.

It's incredibly foggy on Friday morning, the day of our first race, and we eat breakfast nervously in the hotel lobby. The guys race a day after us, so they have today off, and have a slalom race tomorrow. The race has already been delayed an hour, and the fog has hardly cleared. But when Rocco returns from a coaches' meeting, he says that the race is going forward and the chair lifts will still run. Weather conditions aren't as concerning for slalom races because racers don't get going as fast. The gates are really close together, and it's considered the most technical discipline.

My strength is speed, not technique, so my best event is downhill, where the gates are so far apart that our line down the hill is almost straight, and the slope is super steep.

Personally, I'm happy it's foggy. I like racing in bad weather. Maybe it's because there's so much bad weather in Vermont, where I grew up skiing, at least compared to Colorado, where I've been training all season. I like the extra challenge that comes with the bad weather.

Since slalom is my worst discipline, my bib number is higher than usual; the top-ranked racers go first. We've been training on the same courses as the other racers these past two days, and it's intimidating, to say the least. I've never been surrounded by so many elite skiers at once, and the coaches all shout at their athletes in different languages. I never know if the other racers speak English, so there's minimal communication.

It feels like I'm waiting forever to get to the starting gate. Instead of clearing, the fog continues to build until I can barely see the course below. Some of the coaches are pulling out their racers, saying it's too risky and the race should be cancelled. But three of the five Stark girls, Petra, Ingrid, and Sydney, have already raced the first of the two runs we do today, and Lia doesn't seem at all inclined to pull me and Sofia out. I'm relieved at her stance on this, because it'd be a huge letdown to get a DNS (did not start) next to my name on my very first race in Europe.

My name and number are called, and I slide forward to the starting gate while Lia pulls the heavy coat off my shoulders. I've been going over the course in my head for the last hour as the girls ahead of me raced, and I have the line I'll take through the gates memorized. Still, as I stand at the starting gate looking ahead, it's flustering to realize I can only see the very first gate through the whiteout.

I'm just going to have to trust my memory instead of relying on my vision. My legs kick back my skis and I zoom forward out of the gate, pulling hard with my arms to gain maximum momentum before turning through the first gate. My body leans forward as my skis shift confidently back and forth, falling into the rhythm I played over and over in my head. Overthinking my line and second-guessing myself is usually my greatest weakness with slalom, but with the inability to see past the gate in front of me, there's no opportunity to overanalyze. I'm too disoriented to do anything but rely on my rhythm and my memory of the course. The disorientation is something I embrace, because it reminds me of downhill and Super-G, when I'm going so fast that I can't hesitate for even a second. It's all or nothing. Go with the flow or crash.

So I go with it.

My heart races with adrenaline as my shins snap against one gate after another. Slalom gates have never felt so natural, so easy. Maybe I should wear a blindfold from now on. When I pass through the finish line, I don't even have to hear the announcer to know that I raced well.

My downhill race two weeks ago was a shock to the ski world, and I knew I'd get attention at my next downhill and Super-G races, which are in the "speed" disciplines, as opposed to slalom and GS, which are considered "technical" disciplines. But no one expected me to do anything spectacular in the slalom, least of all myself. It's always been the discipline I just survive and get through, trying to do well enough not to ruin my overall FIS points, but knowing it will never be my strength.

There's an official at the bottom to show me how to get out of the netted course finish area. The fog is even thicker down here, but there are still people cheering. I can hear them, if not see them. They must be relying on the commentators because this race isn't quite big enough for televisions and cameras, and I doubt they can see the course.

My time moves me into tenth overall, which might as well be the podium as far as I'm concerned. My bib number is forty-three, which means I came into the race with forty-two women seeded ahead of me. I know some racers dropped out, but only a half-dozen or so, not enough to make this kind of difference. Tenth place in my worst event is awesome.

I find my way to Rocco, who's waiting outside the finish area, and he takes my skis. He's proud of me. "You must have been really paying attention during that inspection run, Roxie," he tells me after a hug.

We only get an hour to check out the course beforehand, and we don't even get to ski through the gates, just look at them. I'd known that memorizing a line would be essential to making it through, if the fog remained, and I'm grateful for all the training I did to prep for today. We've spent so many hours inspecting practice courses back at Stark at the crack of dawn, I've gotten really good at internalizing and visualizing before running a course. At least, that's what my run today tells me.

"Head on into the lodge to warm up. I'll be there in a minute to talk to everyone. The guys are there as well." We'll have a brief team meeting over a quick lunch before the course is set for the next run and we do it all over again. As I'm walking away from the crowd, I hear the commentator announce a crash.

Crashes happen frequently, but I stop in my tracks. Chelsea was two racers after me. Slalom is her best event, and she was psyched for today. We had purposefully kept to ourselves this morning in order to stay focused, but I knew she was up there waiting by the start with me.

"Chelsea Radner is down. This is the sixth skier to crash today, and I'm sure officials are second-guessing their decision to open the race in this weather."

My heart sinks, knowing how horrible she must feel. We've all crashed before, and it always sucks, but doing it at a race like this one is even worse. She's in Chamonix, France, racing her best event at the most competitive FIS race she's ever been at, and it's her very first run. She'll have to scratch the next run. The only consolation is that it's slalom, and she wasn't going fast enough to cause serious injury.

I turn around, though I'm not sure what I intend on doing. Maybe I'll catch her on her way down.

"Roxie?" I hear Brad say my name through the fog, and spot him standing near the bottom of the course.

"Hey, did you hear that announcement?" I ask.

Tyler's right behind him. They have the day off today and they're not dressed in ski gear, just jeans, winter boots, parkas and hats.

"Yeah," Tyler says tightly.

The commentator speaks up again. "Looks like there's going to be a delay on the course. Chelsea Radner, from Sugarville Academy, is having difficulty standing up. The medic team is loading her into a sled to help her down the mountain."

Tyler looks like he might be sick. Another commentator gives a play by play. "She caught a tip on one of the gates and it spun her around backward. It looks like it was an awkward angle, and she may have twisted something. She's moving and sitting up, so that's a good sign."

I take Tyler's gloved hand in my mittened one. "It's okay, Ty. She wasn't going very fast. It can't be very serious."

He nods but doesn't say anything. We huddle together like that, waiting for more news, but the next announcement is that the race has been cancelled. The three of us share shocked glances. I've never heard of a race being cancelled when the first run is almost through like this. Maybe with small, insignificant races, but never a big FIS event.

"Fuck," Tyler growls, kicking his foot in the snow. "They could have made that decision one racer sooner. Just one racer."

"Relax, Tyler," I try not to sound patronizing, but his reaction is a little out of character. "It's probably nothing." I actually don't know if that's true. It's pretty unusual to get pulled down in a sled for a minor injury.

"Six girls crashed," Brad says, shaking his head. "I don't know why they went forward."

"They thought it was going to clear up. I guess that's what usually happens." I don't know why I'm defending the decision. I'm not, I guess, just trying to explain it. Besides, my worry for Chelsea is mixed with disappointment that I won't get to do another run. Without finishing the race, my results won't count. When I see a skier wearing a red medic jacket coming down with a sled behind him, I forget all about the stupid race.

Chelsea must spot us and say something to the medic, because he slows to a stop in front of us. One of my former coaches from Sugarville, Dillon, is with them.

Tyler races up to her and crouches down. Again, that strange sensation hits me. For the first time ever, I can relate to their feelings for each other, and it disarms me. I have the peculiar urge to cry, but I swallow it down.

The medic explains that he's bringing her to the clinic, and he points in that direction. We can just make out the Red Cross sign, and we follow him over there. Chelsea's taken off her helmet, and I can see her cheeks are wet with tears as the medic and Tyler hoist her up to help her inside. They're basically carrying her, which means something hurts too much to walk. Not good. Not good at all.

The clinic is too small to fit all of us, and Brad puts an arm around me and leads me to a hallway with a bench just outside.

"Hey, that was quite the run, Roxie. I know there's more important things to worry about, but I don't want to ignore what you just did out there."

"Thanks," I say, meaning it.

"Sucks it won't be official, but *you* know it happened. It's a huge step for you, isn't it? If you can rock slalom, your least favorite, then you're capable of anything."

I smile at the way he says "least favorite" instead of "worst." Brad's a tactful guy.

"Capable of anything, huh?"

He leans into me, nudging my shoulder. "I'm glad all your hard work at Stark is paying off, Rox, even if we miss you like crazy at home."

I don't know what to say to that. So much has changed since he came to visit me at Stark over Thanksgiving, and since I was home for Christmas break. There was even a moment when I thought things between me and Brad could change this summer. That was when I was planning on returning to Vermont for my senior year. Man, was that only a couple weeks ago?

A burst of cold air hits us when the side door opens, and two skiers walk inside. Even through his ski gear, I recognize Theodore Black, or Ted, as he introduced himself to me months ago. What is he doing here?

Brad met Ted Black as well, when we were all at the Black home for a Thanksgiving party, but he doesn't seem to register who's about to walk past us. My shock doubles when the man stops in front of us, and his eyes lock on mine. He recognizes me.

"Roxanne Slade, right?" he asks, smiling warmly.

"Oh, yes, hi Mr. Black."

"Saw your Stark race suit," he explains, "and I just caught part of your run. Great racing out there."

"Oh, thanks."

I stand up, trying to be polite, and introduce him to Brad, reminding him they met at the Thanksgiving party.

"Oh, a friend of Roxanne's from Sugarville. How nice you're all competing over here together at the same race." I don't know if Ted has an exceptional memory like his son, or of if he's just read the

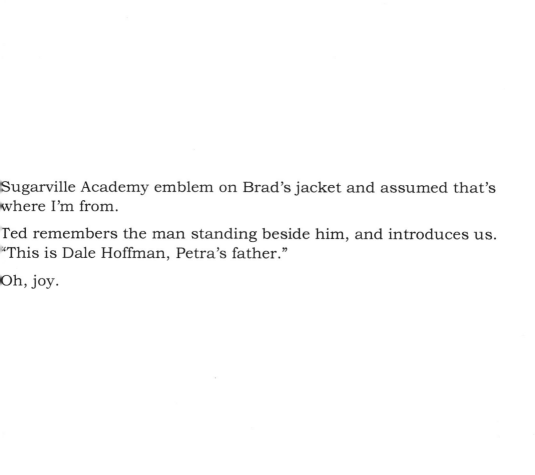

Sugarville Academy emblem on Brad's jacket and assumed that's where I'm from.

Ted remembers the man standing beside him, and introduces us. "This is Dale Hoffman, Petra's father."

Oh, joy.

# Chapter 10

"It's nice to meet you, Roxie, I've heard a lot about you." We shake hands, and my mind is reeling. He's heard a lot about me? WTF? As he turns to Brad, I remember that Aspen's and Winter's parents called Ryker after the falling out, and that he was expecting to hear from Petra's dad at some point too. But what had he said? That he wasn't as pushy?

The man certainly has a presence, more so than Ted Black.

Brad is on his best behavior, because Dale Hoffman is the men's head coach for *the team*. Getting on the U.S. National Team, or just "the team," as we call it, is every ski racer's dream.

"Are you here for the Sugarville racer who crashed? How's she doing?"

Brad answers, "We don't know yet, but he brought her in on a sled, so it might not be good."

Coach Hoffman shakes his head. "It could happen in any race, but that fog was too much. Not a good situation."

We take a few minutes to reflect on the strange morning, how everyone assumed the fog would lift and it didn't, and the controversial decision to cancel mid-race. There will be some angry racers and coaches, but it will blow over. It has to.

"I didn't think the team would be at this race," Brad asks. "Are you here to watch Petra?"

Coach Hoffman nods. "The team flies over next week for the Europa Cup, but I came a few days early to watch Petra race."

"We're headed over to meet up with the Stark team now," Ted says. "Would you like to join us, Roxanne, or are you going to wait for your friend?"

That's right, we were going to have a team meeting. But now the race is cancelled, so I probably don't need to be there. "I think I'll stay here for Chelsea."

"Great to see you, Roxanne, Brad," Ted says with a friendly nod. He's all gentle and serene. Nothing like Ryker. Although he is the only other person who calls me by my full name.

When the men are out of earshot, Brad remarks, "Coach Hoffman looks nothing like his daughter."

"He also seems a lot nicer. Genuinely nice, actually."

Both men are markedly different from their children, come to think of it. Brad chuckles. "Makes you wonder about her mom."

"I've seen photos of Nadia Hoffman and Petra's a carbon copy." Both are gorgeous.

"Why's Ryker's dad here?" Brad wonders.

"No clue. I wanted to ask, but didn't want to be rude."

"You can ask Ryker."

"Yeah, I will," I say, trying to sound breezy. I wonder if Brad is trying to test me, get a feel for how serious Ryker and I are, whether we're talking overseas. "His dad's never at their house in Stark," I add, and maybe to let him know that yeah, I've been spending time at Ryker's place. I don't actually *want* to talk about Ryker with Brad, but I feel like I need to send the message that this thing with Ryker is for real.

Dillon, the Sugarville coach, walks out of the clinic and looks down the hallway. He nods when he sees us. "They're transferring her to the hospital in town. She needs x-rays."

"Where? What do they think it is?" I ask.

Dillon grimaces, and my stomach turns. "Her knee twisted."

Brad glances at me, and we share the same look of fear. Knee injuries are the worst. Even relatively minor ones can weaken the area and set skiers up for future injury. Knees ruin a racing career unlike anything else. A broken bone is often a better diagnosis.

"How is she?" I ask. Dillon knows what I mean.

"She's okay. You know Chelsea. I think the initial shock of the fall and the pain was rough, but she's calming down with Tyler in there with her."

Dillon gestures for us to head into the clinic while he waits outside. It's a tiny space, and Chelsea is propped up on an exam table.

Her lips tremble a little when she says, "Hey, guys."

"Hey, Chels."

She tells us how it happened, how she mistimed a turn and hit the gate too late, catching a ski tip. She was skiing blind, so it's easy to imagine how it happened.

"I'm so sorry, Chels." It's all I can say. There's not much else. Brad echoes the sentiment.

"I know," she says on a sigh. "It's part of the life, right? Gotta roll with the punches and all that." Chelsea tries to shake it off, but I know she's struggling. We all know knees are the worst.

Tyler rubs her back, and then an ambulance arrives to take her to the hospital a few miles away. No siren or anything, but watching a friend get hauled off into an ambulance is a little traumatizing no matter the circumstances.

Tyler hops in with her and Brad puts an arm around me as we watch the ambulance drive off.

"Come on, you should get out of those boots."

I look down at myself. I'm still wearing my race suit and ski boots. "I'll have to go back to the hotel, I didn't leave any at the lodge." The hotel is so close that I've been using it as home base instead of the lodge.

"Let's change and get something to eat. They shut the lifts down," Brad says, nodding in the direction of the chair lift, though we can't see it anymore through the fog. "We won't be skiing any more today, and I'm sure your coaches will just want you resting."

I feel pretty distant from everything as we walk through the village to the hotel. The upcoming races seem so far away, irrelevant really, when my best friend is in the hospital, possibly finding out that her future as a ski racer is permanently jeopardized.

"They'd know right away if it was like, an ACL tear or something really serious, right?" I ask Brad as we step inside my hotel.

Brad pauses before answering. It's a silly question, I know, but I want someone to reassure me. Brad is willing to play along. "Yeah – I mean, she didn't seem to be in excruciating pain. It's probably just a little sprain or something. She might be out for a couple weeks, which sucks since it's only the first day of the circuit, but she'll probably be back up before the end of the season."

Except, this is the end of the season for most of us. There's the U.S. Nationals a couple weeks after we return, but it's pretty unlikely any of us will be invited.

My room's on the third floor of the hotel, and I'm too lazy to take the stairs wearing my heavy ski boots. The elevator is this tiny thing, barely big enough for two people. It's not exactly a Hilton kind of hotel, with more focus on the charm than amenities. We squeeze in together, and I know that Ryker wouldn't be pleased if he were to see how close we have to be to each other. Whatever, it's not like it means anything. But when the doors open, Sven is walking up the staircase, and he sees us tumble out of the elevator.

Sven studies my reaction, and even though I really shouldn't feel guilty, I probably look it, since I was just thinking about how Ryker might react to seeing the lack of space in that elevator.

"Hey, man," Brad greets him, oblivious to the thoughts I can see racing through Sven's head.

"Hi." Sven's reply is curt as his eyes dance between us. "You missed the team meeting," he tells me.

"Chelsea crashed and was brought down in a sled. We went to the clinic with her," I explain. "She's at the hospital now, but I was about to change before grabbing lunch. Want to join us?"

"That sucks," he says, and it sounds heartfelt, but then he asks, "Brad was going to come into your room while you changed?"

"I guess. I can change in the bathroom with the door closed, Sven."

Brad catches onto what Sven is thinking and he lets out an awkward laugh, which doesn't help. "Dude, we've been friends since kindergarten. I'm not about to try anything with her when she's got a boyfriend."

I suppress a groan. *When she's got a boyfriend?* That implies he would try, otherwise. Actually, he has in the past, but only when drunk.

Sven crosses his arms and says, "I'd feel better about this if Brad waited downstairs. Or he can wait in my room."

Brad laughs. He thinks Sven's joking. He's not joking. Ryker probably even told him to keep an eye on Brad, which is why he's acting all pushy. The realization angers me.

"Don't be a jerk, Sven. We're friends. All three of us."

I turn to Brad, who's frowning as it sinks in that Sven isn't messing around. "Just wait downstairs so Sven doesn't get heartburn over it. I'll be down in five."

Sven watches as Brad brushes by him to take the stairs. We're all tense, and it feels like Ryker and his domineering presence are right here with us in Chamonix, France, even though he's basically on the opposite side of the globe in Vancouver right now.

With Brad gone, Sven turns back to me. "We're meeting in the lobby at six tonight for a team dinner. It's with Coach Hoffman and Ted Black. Don't be late." He goes into his room and slams the door, making me feel like an eight-year-old who just got scolded. And why? Because I missed the team meeting to be there for a friend who got hurt? Or because I was seen with one of my best friends, and Sven's been assigned the duty of making sure Brad maintains his distance? Sven's still acting like a bodyguard around me when it comes to Petra, and with the encounter just now, it makes me think maybe Sven and I aren't friends at all. Maybe he's nothing more than Ryker's little soldier.

I'd call Ryker, but it's the middle of the night in Vancouver, and he's competing when he wakes up. Besides, what would I say? I could tell him about the race, Chelsea, his dad, but what would I say about what Sven thinks he saw? Is he going to say something to Ryker about it? Should I defend myself before he can make it sound worse? It's not even a big deal. Or it shouldn't be.

I remember how hurt and vulnerable Ryker looked the night before I left, and how we didn't communicate for two days afterward. He asked me not to keep things from him, even things he won't like, because it makes him wonder what else I'm hiding. It's a trust thing, and his request was a fair one. I'll tell him what happened, so it doesn't backfire like last time.

# Chapter 11

I shouldn't be surprised that the team dinner is at a fancy restaurant. Thankfully, fancy in a ski town doesn't mean chandeliers and waiters in tuxes. I'm wearing jeans and a sweater, which is still a step up from the sweats and hoodies I've been hanging out in after skiing.

I end up sitting between Sven and Ted, directly across from Petra, who's got her dad and Rocco on either side of her. I already know this dinner is going to be painful, and Rocco makes sure of it when he starts off addressing me.

"Roxie, you missed the team meeting today. I told you where to go immediately after your race and we were expecting you."

I tell him about Chelsea, expecting him to back off. I mean really, the race was cancelled. I'm sure he still wants to talk to me about my race, debrief and plan for GS on Sunday, but he had all afternoon to talk to me, didn't he? Maybe he was too busy helping take down the course or at coaches' meetings to go over what happened today, but still. Does he have to do this right now? With an audience?

Petra looks mighty satisfied when Rocco says, "I'm sorry about your friend's crash, Roxie, but that's not a valid excuse. People crash all the time, and she's no longer your teammate. You're a Stark athlete, and your loyalties should be to Stark first."

I sit in stunned silence for a beat. I shouldn't be shocked by the over-the-top attitudes of the Stark coaches, or anyone at Stark, at this point, but Rocco's lack of sympathy is disconcerting. I thought I'd proven myself, shown my dedication and my worth at Stark. But here I am, getting called out about loyalties in front of my team captains. Not to mention my boyfriend's dad and the U.S. National Team coach.

It's tempting to lash out at Rocco and challenge him like I would if this was Ryker talking to me, but by the time I recover from the shock, it's too late. Besides, I'm not sure what I would say.

I'm thrown for another loop when Petra's dad saves me. "Well, I couldn't see much out there, but from what I *could* see, Stark is lucky to have a racer like you, Roxie. You've got some real spunk," he adds, with a shake of his head. "Most racers were pretty conservative today, with the visibility factor, but you attacked those gates with guts. I was impressed."

I blink a few times, amazed by the praise. This is Dale Hoffman, a man who trains the best racers in the nation. Any compliment from him is a meaningful one, and that was... well, that was quite the compliment.

"Thank you." Because really, what else can I say to that?

My eyes skirt to Petra, whose Cheshire cat smile from Rocco's lecture has morphed into a sneer. Yeah, annoyance doesn't even begin to describe her reaction. Rocco doesn't look the least bit surprised, which makes me wonder if he agrees with the praise. *He's* never said anything like that to me before.

The conversation moves on to the repercussions of cancelling the race today, the weather forecast for tomorrow (better), and what we can expect for the GS courses on Sunday and Monday.

When we're through with dinner and I still haven't heard anything about why Ted Black is here in France, I break from ski talk to turn to him. "Are you here to watch the competitions, Mr. Black?"

"Please, call me Ted. And yes, I'll probably try to catch some of the races, but I have a house here in Chamonix. I'm here a lot in the winter. Most of the winter, actually."

"Oh." What do I say to that? "I didn't know that. Do you speak French?"

He smiles. "Yes. I studied abroad in France in college. Do you have any interest in foreign languages?"

"Not really. I took the mandatory Spanish classes, but aside from Canada, I've never left the States before this week. Didn't give me a lot of motivation to learn a second language."

He nods as I speak. "Yes, and in Europe nowadays, English has become the common language, particularly in tourist spots."

I end up chatting with Ryker's dad for a while about traveling in Europe, which is weird, since I know nothing. The man seems to enjoy giving me insight into the places I'll be traveling on this trip. He's a hard man to read, though. Or maybe not at all. There's just not as much to him as I would've expected from someone related to Ryker Black. He's pretty even-keeled and steady. Behind his kindness and friendliness, I can sense that there's a lack of strength. Ryker once told me his father was weak, but it's not Ryker's words that make me draw this opinion. There's just no spark to Ted Black, no fire inside him. He's certainly not a natural leader.

When we all stand up to head out, Rocco asks me to stay. "We haven't had a chance to talk about your race this morning," he explains.

It makes me wonder why he didn't wait to bring up the team meeting if he was planning on keeping me anyway. Did he want an audience for that?

We sit at the empty table while the waiter clears plates, and Rocco asks how the race felt today. I forget about my agitation with him as I relay my mindset, how I relied on my memory of the course and didn't second-guess myself.

"I just hope I can remember that feeling of getting into a rhythm and going with it."

But it doesn't feel like Rocco cares much about what I'm saying. His eyes are glazed, like he's thinking about something else. Is he even paying attention to me?

When I stop talking, I wait. Finally, his eyes find mine and he says, "Roxie, I'm concerned about Ryker."

My lungs constrict at his words. "What? Is he okay? What happened?"

"I'm concerned about his commitment to Stark, Inc. and I know the two of you are dating now," he continues, ignoring my frenzied questions.

I am *so* confused. How does he know we're dating? Why does he care about Ryker's commitment to Stark, Inc.? And why is he talking to *me* about it?

Rocco acts like the answers to all of those questions are irrelevant or obvious as he continues, "The past two weeks, Ryker's made some moves with the company that raise red flags. People think he might be setting things up for a replacement. Someone new to take over as CEO."

"I didn't know you were involved in the company," I say quietly.

"I've been on the Stark, Inc. board for almost six years," he replies, as if I should know this fact. It doesn't make sense to me. He's a ski coach. I can't even imagine him wearing a suit and tie and sitting behind a computer.

"Why are you talking to me about this?"

"Because Ryker started making changes the week before we left for this trip, and I know things got serious between you two right before that."

My expression must convey that I find Rocco's knowledge about my personal life a little disturbing, because he adds, "It was on national television, Roxie. Everyone was talking about it."

I keep forgetting that. Still, this conversation is weirding me out.

"Yeah, I know, but what do *I* have to do with Stark, Inc.?"

Rocco leans back in his chair and clasps his hands in front of him. "I'm concerned that he's backing out of his responsibilities, giving up the position he's sacrificed so much for, because of you."

And there it is. An accusation.

I am furious.

"Rocco, you are my ski coach. That is it. I don't know why you think you have a right to talk to me about my boyfriend, or why you think you have any right to comment on *his* personal life, but I don't like it. What are you trying to do here?" I keep my voice even, and I'm amazed at my self-control. Rocco Moretti was a man I held on a pedestal at the beginning of the school year, and I still respect him. As a coach. He's stepped over a line here.

Rocco changes his tone, softening it to appease me. "But that's what I'm saying, Roxie. His personal life, it seems to me, is impacting the business, and as a member of the board, I do have a right to be concerned about this."

My eyes narrow at his explanation. I'm not buying it.

"I will admit that there is a personal element to my concern, as well. Ryker's mother, Elizabeth Stark, was a close friend of mine. I know that she wanted very much for Ryker to follow in her footsteps. She was concerned that there was no one else in the family who would, or could, fill her position. Of course, she thought he would have years skiing before she started training him in the business, and it would be decades before she retired and passed on the reins, but, well, it didn't work out that way." The deep sadness in his voice as he speaks about her tells me that he cared for Elizabeth Stark, and perhaps that is the main drive behind his worry that her only son might be walking away from her legacy.

"What Ryker has accomplished is truly incredible," Rocco continues, almost reverently. "I wouldn't be the only one to be tremendously disappointed if he chose to step down. Stark, Inc. is in even better shape than when Elizabeth died. People see that, and they won't want him to go."

"I still don't get why you're telling me any of this." It hasn't escaped me that Rocco could be fishing for information, trying to find out what Ryker is up to. I don't know what he means about what "moves" Ryker has made or "red flags" he is raising. Ryker doesn't talk to me about that stuff, and I doubt it's something he could explain without going into loads of detail. But I do know that Ryker intends to step down as CEO, and I can't let that slip.

"I think that you have some influence on him, and that he's likely making these changes for you."

I scoff at that idea, though he's not far from the truth. "We've been together two weeks, Rocco. I didn't *ask* him to do anything with Stark, Inc., if that's what you think. He doesn't even talk to me about that stuff. It's the most important part of snowboarding season, he's probably just busy with that."

Rocco studies me with skepticism.

"Well, I would appreciate it if you would talk to him about it," he finally says. "Remind him of his mother's wishes, and his responsibilities to the Stark legacy. He might listen."

For the second – or is it third? – time tonight, I have the urge to lash out. But I hold back, not wanting to say something I shouldn't, or fall into a trap. He can't really think I'll convince Ryker of anything having to do with Stark, Inc., so all I can guess is that he's setting a trap, trying to get me to tell him what Ryker's up to.

I say nothing, just stand and walk away. He can interpret that however he chooses.

My heart is pounding out of my chest as I make my way back to the hotel. What the hell was that? I try calling Ryker, but he's probably in the middle of competing right now, and it goes straight to voicemail. This isn't something I can explain on a message. So much has happened in the past twelve hours, and I don't know when I'll be able to talk to Ryker again at this point.

Instead, I call Chelsea, who's back at her hotel. She has a grade two MCL sprain. It didn't tear, and she won't need surgery, but she can't ski for two months, which puts her out for the season. I tell her I'm coming over, and I don't give a damn if Rocco thinks I should be going straight to bed. He's the one who crossed a boundary tonight, and in doing so, he lost a large chunk of my respect. If my coach thinks visiting my injured friend is disloyal to Stark, he should reevaluate his priorities.

# Chapter 12

My legs have never been so thoroughly trashed. I raced hard yesterday at the Giant Slalom, earning a top-ten finish in my second-worst discipline, and we got a few training runs in today, after the guys' race. I'm grateful we get the day off for travel to Austria tomorrow. It's Monday night, our last night in Chamonix, and my energy level is at an all-time low.

I've just finished eating dinner with Chelsea, Tyler, Brad, Sven and Ingrid, and Chelsea's trying to convince us to go to a bar. I want to tell her that I'm suffering from bone-deep exhaustion, but I don't want to rub it in her face that I've been racing my ass off while she's been sidelined. She's been a great sport, cheering us on and not complaining, but now she's playing us.

"Guys, come on, I haven't had a chance to do anything fun in this stupid brace. They don't care about your age in France. Let's just have one drink to celebrate your awesome racing."

She makes it impossible to say no.

Other racers must have had the same idea, because the pub is packed with skiers. I recognize some of them, though it's kind of hard to tell since we rarely see each other without goggles and helmets on. We're trying to get close enough to the bar to order drinks when I feel my phone buzz in my back pocket. My heart leaps when I check it. *Ryker*. Finally.

We've been playing phone tag for days. Last time we spoke was Thursday night. Neither of us wanted to interrupt each other's sleep, and with the time differences and busy competition schedules, it's been impossible to connect. His last event was yesterday though, and they're traveling to New Hampshire later today, I think.

"Hey!" I put the phone to my ear, but I can't really hear his response over the noisy bar. "Hang on a sec," I tell him, and push my way back out to the front door.

"Sorry," I say, when the door closes behind me and it's quiet again.

"Where are you?"

"Chelsea guilt-tripped us into going to a bar."

"Guilt-tripped?" he asks, and I remember he doesn't know what's been going on. I tell him about what happened with Chelsea, and then how I saw his dad and Coach Hoffman.

"So much has happened, and man, I miss you," I tell him when I get to the part where the race was cancelled, I missed the team meeting, and Sven thought Brad was coming up to my bedroom for the wrong reasons. It all feels so irrelevant for the moment.

"I miss you too, Roxanne. I hate not knowing everything that's going on." We've been texting about our results, and he knows that I've been rocking my races, while he placed third at the Big Air competition. But we haven't had a chance to just talk, and now I have all this crap to unload on him.

The door of the pub opens and Brad pokes his head out. He sees me on the phone and mouths, "Ryker?" I nod, and he goes back inside.

"Hey, have you talked to Sven at all in the past few days?" I ask.

"We've texted a few times, why?"

That doesn't tell me if Sven's been spying on me and reporting back to Ryker, but it wouldn't surprise me if he had, whether or not Ryker specifically asked him to. Sighing, I tell him how Sven saw Brad and me get out of the elevator and acted all suspicious.

"It wasn't anything, but I wanted to tell you because of what you said before, that if I keep things from you, you'll think I'm hiding other things too."

There's a long pause on the other end before Ryker says, "You are only telling me this because you thought Sven would say something to me about it, aren't you?" It's not meant as an accusation, I don't think. He's genuinely curious. I can't hear any emotion in his voice, but for some reason, I'm picturing that expression he had at the top of the stairs the night before we left.

"Partly, yeah. I mean, I wouldn't have told you anything because it *wasn't* anything, Ryker. Honestly, I didn't even think about it until I saw how weird Sven was acting."

"That's the thing that worries me sometimes, Roxie. You don't have an ounce of scandal in you. There's nothing conniving in your nature, and I worry that could get you in trouble. There's a lot of malice in my world, and if you aren't thinking like someone with malice, you might not even realize what's happening."

"Um, are we still talking about Brad? He's not malicious, Ryker."

"Maybe not, but think about what those girls did to you on that mountain, Roxanne."

"Hey," I interrupt then, "I had a feeling they were up to something and I had my guard up. But you can't blame me for not seeing *that* coming."

There's another pause. "There's a lot at stake here," he says quietly. "Especially with me stepping down. Someone else will be taking my place, and people are starting to get antsy. They sense change. I don't want you to worry about appearances all the time, but be careful, okay?"

"Yeah, I will be." It's a little unclear what he's getting at, but I think back to how Rocco pinned me with all that crap, and how weird it was.

"I'm not as worried about Brad as I was back in the fall. I know you're with me now, and I wasn't sure where we stood back then. I wanted you, but didn't think I could have you. At least, not in the way that meant you were mine alone. I trust you, Roxanne, okay? And I know he's not a bad guy."

"Then why all the scary warnings?"

"The truth?"

"Duh."

"Brad wants you, and he also wants what's best for you. Whether he's right or not, he might not think that I'm what's best for you, and he might convince himself it's his duty as your friend to get you out of this relationship."

"That's a pretty convoluted analysis of the situation, Ryker."

"People convince themselves of all kinds of things when they want something badly enough."

"Wait, are you talking about Brad or yourself? I'm confused."

He laughs softly. "I just miss you and I'm worrying more than I should. Is that what you wanted to get off your chest? That and seeing Coach Hoffman and my father, I mean."

"Actually, there's one more thing."

The front door opens again, and this time it's Sven who walks out. "Everything okay?" he asks.

"Yeah, just on the phone with Ryker."

"Oh, tell him I said hi." I nod and he goes back inside.

"Who was that?"

"Sven. Did you tell him to keep an eye on me?" I'm about to say Brad's already on it, but realize that would be a stupid thing to say.

"Back at Beaver Creek when you first told me what had happened with the princesses, but he knows I'd want him to keep doing it."

Good, it doesn't sound like he gave him specific instructions about Brad or anything. That would be a little bit overbearing, if not entirely unexpected from Ryker.

I tell Ryker about my strange conversation with Rocco. "You know, I'm not totally oblivious to people's agendas, because I sensed something was off. Yeah, I trusted him as my coach, but I got the sense he wasn't just talking to me because he wanted me to change your mind, remind you of your legacy, or whatever. I think he was fishing for info."

"Probably, but he's also obsessed with the legacy too." Ryker doesn't sound too concerned. He doesn't like that I was approached about it, but he doesn't seem to think Rocco's up to anything sinister.

I don't know, it felt awfully strange to me, but maybe that's only because I didn't know Rocco had any involvement in Stark, Inc. or was such close friends with Ryker's mother. It threw me for a loop.

Neither of us wants to get off the phone, but it's been nearly half an hour and I'm freezing. Besides, I should have that drink with Chelsea that I promised.

When we say goodbye, there's this odd moment when it feels like the word "love" might slip out of either of our mouths. Maybe I just imagined it, on his end at least. Because that would be crazy, right? There's no way we can feel that kind of big emotion already, is there? We've only been together a short time, but it feels like so much longer than that. Like, maybe there was a relationship forming even before Beaver Creek, even when we weren't talking to each other. Now I'm just being crazy. Love is a deep thing, and I've seen it misplaced or misidentified with so many girls my age. I really need to get a handle on myself.

It takes a while to find my friends in the pub. A few people stop me and try to start a conversation, and I have to figure out a polite way to brush them off. The thing is, I bet there are a lot of interesting ski racers here tonight, and it'd be cool to chat with them in this context, without skis on and a course looming between us. But there will be more opportunities for that.

My friends are hanging by the back wall at a high-top table, and I immediately notice that Ingrid and Sven are very close together. Like, coupley-together. When I approach, I can't help myself. Wagging a finger between them, I ask, "Did I miss something? When did this happen?"

Ingrid glances down at her hands, but Sven answers, "You didn't miss anything, Slade. But hey, any chance you want to bunk with Chad tonight so I can have your room?"

My eyes aren't the only ones bulging. Ingrid swings her head from Sven, to me, to my Vermont friends, who are cracking up. "Um, no? You're kidding, right?" He wants me to sleep in his room with his roommate?

"Uh, yeah. Ryker would kill me."

"For hooking up with me?" Ingrid asks, not quite catching on.

He squeezes her closer. "No, he'd be down with that. For having his girl share a room with Chad so I could hook up with you."

"Oh."

Tyler says, "Brad's had his own room since we did some rearranging."

"Unless he's planning on meeting a girl at the pub tonight, you mean," Chelsea teases.

"Yeah, Ryker would be even more pissed about Roxie staying with Brad than he would if it was Chad," Sven says.

"He doesn't have to know," Chelsea dismisses Sven's concern, like it's no big deal. "They have their own beds, but those two have shared a bed at parties plenty of times. Oh wait, yeah, bad idea. I forgot about how pissed Ryker got when the two of you were going to crash in the same bed over Thanksgiving."

Fortunately, Tyler changes the subject, but this is another one they aren't entirely clued in on. He turns to Brad, "Dude, is Petra still all over you? She wants you." I can feel Ingrid and Sven looking at me when Tyler glances between the three of us, asking, "You guys wouldn't care if that happened, right?"

Chelsea shoves her boyfriend. "Ty, you can be so clueless sometimes. Haven't you noticed Petra doesn't hang out with us like she did over Thanksgiving? And she was pretty snobby then."

"So she's not friends with you guys anymore. What's the big deal? Brad hooks up with girls who aren't friends of ours all the time. Actually, he basically exclusively hooks up with non-friends."

Brad groans. "I'm standing right here, man. And no, I don't want Petra. She's too annoying."

Phew. I did not want to be put in the position of talking him out of that. I don't even know how I'd explain it.

Still, the entire conversation is surprisingly not that awkward, given the subject matter. I like how the six of us have formed this easy comradery, where we can talk about switching sleeping arrangements for hookups, and laugh about Ryker's reaction to it. The only thing is that it now seems Brad and I are the only non-couple.

As we walk back to our hotels, Ingrid and Sven walk ahead, arms around each other. They'll get their time in a hotel room together soon enough. I'm not about to sleep in the hallway for them.

Tyler and Chelsea are behind them, walking cautiously with Chelsea's knee still fragile. She leans into him, and he supports her weight.

Naturally, Brad and I walk together. I can't help but wonder what he's thinking. Does he wish I would lean into him? It's what I would've done before Ryker. I wouldn't have even thought about it and even now it's hard not to do it on instinct. But Ryker told me he trusted me, and I want to deserve that trust.

Chapter 13

We settle into our hotel in Austria on Tuesday afternoon. We'll train on Wednesday, and then we have another round of slalom and GS races, just like in France, beginning on Thursday, with the guys. It isn't until we get to Italy that we'll race downhill and Super-G, my favorites. The speed disciplines are logistically really tough on resorts, in terms of coordinating with everyone else who wants to ski the mountain. A downhill course has to be very long and very steep, which means it takes away a significant portion of the mountain's terrain from those who just want to ski. Plus, there have to be multiple training days before we can even race, so racers basically take over the mountain for a week.

As I wander around the mountain village, checking things out and stretching my legs, I notice a lot more snowboarders than I did in Chamonix. Player and Ryker compete in freestyle, as opposed to alpine snowboarding, which is about speed and involves stiffer boots and boards, more like skiing. Freestyle has three disciplines: half-pipe, slopestyle, and big air. Ryker's strongest is half-pipe and my eyes roam over to the giant walls of snow taking up half the trail near the base of the mountain.

Half-pipes look, well, like half of a giant pipe, made of snow. Riders, or skiers, slide up one side, catch air when the wall ends, and slide back down, only to go back up the other side and repeat. In competitions, they do flips and stuff in the air. I tried going through the half-pipe at Sugarville once, and I got so dizzy I almost threw up. And that was only going halfway up the wall. I didn't even catch air.

I walk over to the bottom of the pipe to watch people coming down. Half-pipes are usually at the base of resorts for just this purpose – so people can watch. Especially for competitions. Ryker hasn't really talked about his goals, how far he wants to go. I know he's not on the World Cup circuit yet, the highest level of snowboarding, but he had been on the podium at every one of his FIS competitions this year. FIS isn't just for alpine skiing, but the organization also covers snowboarding and all the other forms of skiing (Nordic, freestyle, jumping, speed racing, and telemark). I've heard Player mention "the team" and I know that making the National Team is the ultimate goal for snowboarders at Stark, just like it is for the skiers. I think the Snowboarding National Team members are picked by discipline, and I wonder if Ryker wants to be on it. Is that a goal of his that he's never verbalized or maybe never even acknowledged to himself? As I watch people go through the half-pipe and imagine what Ryker can do when he catches air, I have to think that his decision to step down from Stark, Inc. was driven by his gift on a snowboard.

Ryker's parents groomed him for alpine ski racing, and he didn't even start riding until he was twelve years old, but he's already rising to the top.

"Roxie?" I turn around at the sound of my name.

"Hey," I say to the familiar face. "How's it going, Carter?" Carter Leduc was my first kiss, years ago, but I hardly know the guy. He's on the Canadian National Team, and I ran into him at Beaver Creek a couple of weeks ago.

"We just got in this morning, how about you?"

Carter backed off from hitting on me when he learned Ryker was with me, or actually, when Ryker warned him away. He's friendly, but not *too* friendly, this time around.

We catch up for a couple minutes, and then he asks me about Ingrid. "Oh, yeah, she's here." I almost add, *I think she's making out with Sven Teslow at the moment.* Ingrid had a little crush on Carter when we were at Beaver Creek, and though I don't think it escalated past flirting, I could see it going further, if Sven weren't in the picture. I'm not sure what's happening with Sven and Ingrid though so I'm staying out of it. Hopefully it won't get complicated.

"Can you tell her I said hi?" He tells me where his team is staying and says we can stop by anytime to hang out. It's the same hotel the Stark team is at, but I don't tell him so. At Beaver Creek, the Canadian Team was the partying team, so this situation could get interesting. Hopefully Ingrid will play it smart and stick to Sven.

A few of Carter's teammates walk by and stop to say hello. When they invite me and my friends to party, I'm not surprised. They must know that Ryker isn't here this time to warn them off. I'm still kind of embarrassed about that. These guys must be on the Canadian C and D teams though, because I think that the Canadian A and B teams are at the Europa Cup right now.

I end up telling them we're at the same hotel as them since they're going to find out anyway. Besides, I'm ready to head back there, since I forgot to bring my cell and I want to call my parents. Ryker's probably in New Hampshire now, and he wakes up at the crack of dawn so I can try him, too.

When we walk into the hotel lobby, a familiar back with a Stark jacket is standing at the check-in counter. Familiar but... not supposed to be here.

"Player?" I ask.

He looks behind him and his eyes go wide before he flashes one of his easy smiles. "Hey Rox, surprised to see me?"

"Uh, yeah, what are you doing here?"

"What kind of greeting is that?" he asks, opening his arms for a hug. I relent and walk into them, but I'm super confused. "There's a half-pipe competition on Sunday when the ski races wrap up. Ryker thought we could use some tougher competition before the national championships in Utah in a couple weeks so he sent us, I mean me, he registered me for the event. No one else on the team is here."

I narrow my eyes suspiciously. Ryker Black is pulling a stunt on me. I know it.

"Who are your friends, Roxie?" He's looking behind my shoulder and I turn around to find five guys on the Canadian National team staring at us.

As they start introducing themselves, the guys don't deny that they are my friends, which annoys me. But I'm not really paying any attention. I want to know where Ryker is. I know he's here. He has to be. But then I remember that I don't have my phone, and he could be looking for me.

I spin around, planning to rush upstairs to my room to grab it, and I hit a hard chest. I look up, and there he is. My arms immediately wrap around his neck and I just can't hold back, I jump right into his arms. My legs wrap around his waist and I laugh as I kiss him. I am *so* one of *those* girls. And it feels good. Damn good.

"Roxanne," he whispers into my ear as I finally calm myself down enough to slide back into standing.

My arms remain around his neck though, and his hands stay around my waist as we stare at each other. I can't stop touching him, and it's ridiculous I feel this way, a voice in my head yells. It's only been a week! A week and a day, actually, but whatever.

"We're still here, guys," Player reminds us.

I don't really want to turn around and find the Canadian Team watching this private moment, but I do look over at Player.

"So, who else is here?" I ask them.

"It's just us," Ryker tells me. "The rest of the team is in New Hampshire."

I don't know what to say. He came here for me. Player's here, so it's for the half-pipe event, too, but I know they would be in New Hampshire if not for me. It might not be as hard for Ryker to change his competition schedule and book a last-minute flight to Europe as it is for normal people, but still, this is crazy.

We have a short conversation with Carter and his teammates before they head off to the elevators. Ryker doesn't ask why they were hovering, and it really doesn't even matter, since he's *here*. In Austria.

"You got the keys to our room?" he asks Player.

"Hey! I'm not getting kicked out of our room when I just got here. Go in Roxie's room," Player complains.

"I'm pretty sure Ingrid's in there right now with Sven," I admit.

Player glances at Ryker and then back to me.

Ryker asks, "When did that start happening?"

I look at my watch. "An hour ago."

Player chuckles and Ryker purses his lips, deciding how he feels about this information.

"There was only one room open with all the races here this week. And we were lucky to get that one," Player says. "So, if you want to stay close to the mountain, you're stuck rooming with me."

Player smirks devilishly, knowing that the sleeping arrangements will get switched around soon enough. He loses the confident look when Ryker says, "Go check out the pipe, man. You can come up to the room in half an hour."

Player doesn't argue, just sighs heavily and hands over a key card. "Take my bag up, then." He nods to the bags by the counter and turns to leave.

We're alone. Well, almost. The pretty blonde at the check-in counter looks enthralled by the exchange. Or by Ryker, that's possible too. There was just an abundance of way-above-average hotness in the room a minute ago, so I guess I can't blame her for the wide eyes and rosy cheeks.

Ryker doesn't say anything as he swings one bag over his shoulder and pulls a suitcase behind him with the other, not letting me help.

"When did you get here? Were you waiting for me long?"

"I've only been at the hotel for five minutes. I went to your room while Player checked in. Ingrid answered, and now I know why she was acting weird. Sven's in there, huh?"

"Yup. I got booted." Well, I volunteered to go for a walk during our scheduled "down time."

We step onto the elevator, and even though it's only going up three floors, Ryker leans forward for another kiss. "You should have told Player longer than half an hour," I tell him as we step off the elevator.

"He knows I meant longer than that," he says with a knowing glance in my direction. Ryker's sliding the key card into a door when another one down the hall opens, and Petra walks out. She spots us immediately, and the look on her face is one I won't be forgetting anytime soon.

First there's the eyebrows shooting up in surprise, and her mouth forming a circle. Disbelief flashes first, followed quickly by furrowed brows. Denial. She can't accept that Ryker is here for me. And the next second, rage. That only lasts an instant before she covers it all with a cold mask. But I saw the rage there, and that scared me a little. She might act cool and indifferent as she brushes by us and takes the elevator downstairs, but she's not going to be able to keep the fury contained, I just know it. She'll pull something on me, on us, at some point.

When the elevator doors close behind her, Ryker holds his room door open for me. "She's been staying out of your way, right?"

"So far, yeah. Her dad seems like a nice guy. Not like her at all."

Ryker doesn't respond to that, and when the door shuts behind us, butterflies blast to life in my belly. It hits me that we're alone in a hotel room, with nothing but luggage between us. Why does this feel so much different than when we've been at his house?

# Chapter 14

Even with rumpled clothes from traveling, Ryker looks amazing. He tugs off his winter hat, and soft chestnut hair falls over his forehead. I've tried using the same shampoo he has in his shower at Stark, and my hair never gets as soft as his. I can almost hear the air between us crackle as we watch each other. I wonder if he's studying all my features, checking they are the same as he remembered, the way I am doing to him.

Ryker's the first to break the stare-down. He drops one of the bags, rolls the other one to the side, and sweeps me up in him. He's all around me, hands on my waist, but just breathing, keeping me super close to his body. "Sorry," he says heavily. "I just wanted to be touching you."

I don't get why he's apologizing. It's why he's here, isn't it?

"I can't believe you're here. That you came."

I want him to tell me it was for me, that he couldn't stay away, even if his presence says it already. He doesn't say anything. But he does kiss me. It starts out tender and turns heated fast. I think that might just be the way Ryker operates. There's no in-between for him, it's all or nothing. And maybe that's why we struggled to figure out who we were, what our relationship was, for such a long time.

Before I know it, I'm up against the wall, gripping onto the soft curls at the nape of his neck, my favorite spot. Ryker's lips move along my collarbone and I breathe out, "What is it with you and walls?"

He laughs lightly, slowing things down as he answers. "It wasn't a thing before you, believe me. I'm just afraid to get you horizontal, on a bed or something. It's harder to keep control that way. Things can escalate too fast."

I want to point out that things escalate pretty darn quickly in vertical too, but my mind wants to know why he's holding back. "I want to get on the bed," I tell him, and his eyes meet mine. He knows it's a challenge: move us to the bed or tell me why you won't.

"We slept in the same bed for like, a week straight before I left, and you didn't have a problem with that."

"Yeah, but we were sleeping. Mostly," he adds, remembering all the goodnight kisses that turned into more.

I know he wants me; his body pressed against mine tells me that. He's not hiding it from me either, or he wouldn't have flown across an ocean to see me. Because even if he won't say it outright, I know that's why he's here.

"What am I missing, Ryker? Since the carnival at Beaver Creek, you haven't been holding back with us. Except for this."

Ryker puts a little space between us, though he leaves his hands on my hips. "Isn't it obvious?" He bites his lip, looking genuinely confused.

I shake my head. If it was obvious, I wouldn't be asking.

"You know I've never had a girlfriend. I told you that at the very start."

"Yeah, so? I've never had a boyfriend either. Until you."

"I don't want to talk about how it was before you, but I kind of have to if I'm going to answer your question." He searches my face for permission and I nod. It's not as if I don't already know. "I hooked up with girls, and that's it. We usually had sex, and there was nothing more."

Wow. It feels like he hit me in the chest with a shovel or something. Which is totally dumb, because he basically told me all this before, or my friends did, just not quite so bluntly. Hearing him say it outright is brutal.

"I know it probably isn't fun to hear, but I didn't want a relationship. Most girls wanted more, so I couldn't give any indication I might be up for that, or they'd get confused and it'd be a pain in my ass. That's one of the reasons it was never monogamous and never more than a few times with the same girl."

My eyes drift to our feet. I get what he's saying and I know who he was, who he still is, but it doesn't change that he sounds like an asshole explaining it. I mean really, he's so logical and detached talking about these girls that he shared intimacy with, it's hard not to feel a little sick about it. Ryker uses a finger to lift my chin so I'm looking at him.

"We're different. You're different. Okay? I'm trying to say that, before you, it was all about the sex. And now, it's not about that at all. Or, it hasn't been. I want you like that. Obviously," he says with a little smile. "But that's only a piece of what I want with you, and it's a really insignificant piece, actually. Like, I could do without it and still want to be your boyfriend."

"What if I didn't even want you to kiss me?" I challenge. "Or hold my hand, or get near me?"

Ryker looks confused by my question. "If that was the case, I'd wonder why you wanted to be with me, or if you were afraid of me. I mean, touching you in any way is nice and I know you like it too, but this isn't a physical relationship, and I don't want it to become one."

Only an eighteen-year-old guy like Ryker could say something like that and actually mean it. Any other guy his age, and I wouldn't believe the words coming from his mouth were remotely genuine. I suppose it doesn't hurt that he's had plenty of experience already so it's not like he's eager to prove anything.

"What about what I want?" I ask.

Ryker looks like he's trying to decide whether my question is amusing, offensive, or deeply profound. "Are you saying you just want my body, Roxanne?" He's only half-joking.

"No. I want you as a lot more than that." I try to put as much sincerity into my voice as I can muster. "But I'm not so worried about things changing between us. Maybe I should be, but I just know that I want all of you. Ryker the snowboarder, Ryker the business prodigy, Ryker the king of Stark Springs Academy, and the guy who's figuring out all those things and what they mean to him. I want all of that." Ryker keeps his face neutral, but I know my words are affecting him by the way his eyes soften. And then I add, "I want all of you, with and without clothes on."

His mouth parts and he blinks a few times, and then he closes it again. He needs more encouragement than that? Fine.

"I want to share all of me with you too, Ryker, okay? We have something special and it's why we put up with each other from the beginning, even when we didn't want to like each other. You don't want to give me the piece of you that so many other girls have already had because you think it will undermine us, right?" I don't wait for him to confirm, but go on, "Well, I want to give you a piece of myself that I've never shared with anyone else, and never wanted to. I'm not doing it lightly, either. I'm just saying, I want it to be you, eventually, some day, and I know when it happens, it'll be a big deal for both of us."

I don't know if he grasped anything else I was saying because all he can get out is, "You've never had sex? You're a virgin?"

"Before you, I'd kissed two guys total, and that's it."

I've shocked Ryker even more now, because he just stands there, opening and closing his mouth. Maybe now we really won't touch ever again. Did I freak him out?

"And, you're saying, you want me to be the guy who…" He drifts off, unable to get the words out.

I nod slowly. Yes, Ryker, I want it to be you. Get it through your head. He seems to come to a decision because he stops gaping at me, steps away and crosses his arms.

"That's not going to happen anytime soon. There are a lot of things we need to do before that." He sounds dead serious and I burst into laughter.

"Ryker, this isn't like a checklist thing. We're not in training to reach a goal." He uncrosses his arms, looks affronted at my laughter for a moment, and then he relents with a small smile.

"I know that, Roxanne," he says softly. "For now, I'm exhausted and I want to lie down with you, in the bed."

"I can do that," I agree. The heat between us has cooled off with the conversation, and despite the weightiness of what we just talked about, not to mention the potential awkwardness, I feel totally comfortable crawling under the covers with him. As I lie on his chest, one of his arms on my bottom and the other on my leg that's draped over his, I feel closer to him than I ever have before.

We lie like that, neither of us really sleeping but neither of us fully awake either, for some time. It could be ten minutes or two hours, it's hard to say in this half-awake zone, until Player returns. He calls Ryker to say he's on his way up, and we climb out of bed.

"Do Rocco and Lia know you're here?" I ask.

"Yeah, I emailed them yesterday. You hungry?"

At his question, I remember that I had plans to meet my Vermont friends for dinner, like I have every night. "I'm supposed to go with Chelsea and all them. Ingrid and Sven, too. Did you want to go by ourselves, or..." I let the question drift, uncertain what his stance will be.

"We'll go with your friends," he says decisively. "What's the plan?"

I check my phone for messages just as Player opens the door. "You guys want to get some food? I'm starved."

Chelsea texted me where to meet them, and it's in ten minutes. Ingrid must've gotten the text too, because the elevator stops at her floor on the way down, and she and Sven look super confused when they see me standing between Ryker and Player on the elevator. But they don't ask questions when we tell them about the half-pipe competition on Sunday. We all know that the half-pipe isn't the reason, the real reason, for coming all the way to Austria, but Ryker's a hard guy to tease – at least, in this context.

The same scenario repeats itself when we run into my Vermont friends on the way to dinner, except they are more surprised, and they can't let it go.

"Wait," Chelsea says, "you had a half-pipe event in New Hampshire, but decided this one was more competitive, and it just so happens to be where Roxie is racing?"

"Don't forget they show up on the same day we show up, when their event isn't until Sunday," Tyler adds.

"Is the rest of the team here?" Brad asks.

"Just us," Ryker says easily. He doesn't seem to mind their insinuations.

Player tells us, "Aspen Davies was pissed. We don't usually do a lot of Europe trips, and she wanted in on this one. She qualified and got invited, but the *coaches* told her she was better off at New Hampshire."

I don't know if my Vermont friends pick up on the "coaches" part. I've told them a lot about how things work at Stark, but I'm not sure they realize that Ryker can tell the coaches what to do, and they listen. In a way, he's like their boss, but indirectly.

"She has a chance at hitting the podium in New Hampshire, and it would be a long shot here," Ryker says, like it's totally about strategy. "You and I have a real shot at the podium at both. And yeah, the decision was easy. I made the changes the day the alpine team left. I'd forgotten that we'd been invited to this event months ago. New Hampshire was already on the calendar so I didn't change it, but then I figured, why not? Now I don't have to go an entire three weeks without seeing my girlfriend."

We step into the restaurant then, cutting off the conversation for the moment as we find a table. Ryker's admission doesn't make me feel all warm fuzzy like it should. He's brushing it off like it's no big deal, and I know he's doing that so he doesn't sound too gushy in front of our friends, but it's the timing of it that puts me off, not the way he said it. He's known about this event for a while, before we even got together, but waited until the day after I told him Brad would be here to make the changes. He could have done it any time the week before, and he waited until that day. I know we'd only been together a week, and maybe it wasn't until I left that he realized he would miss me a lot, but still... I can't help but think maybe he doesn't trust me as much as he says he does.

# Chapter 15

Brad is quiet during dinner, and I wonder if it's hard for him to see me with Ryker like this. When we all hung out together over Thanksgiving, Ryker and I weren't acting all coupley, and even now, I'm a little suspicious that Ryker's super-attentiveness to me is a show for Brad. I know he hasn't seen me in over a week, but he's not usually so touchy in front of our friends. And maybe I'm overthinking everything, the timing of his decision to come out here, his jealousy about Brad, and Brad's feelings toward me. Maybe none of it means anything. After all, Brad has never really told me how he feels.

We're finishing our dinner and deciding on dessert when we get another unexpected visitor, and this time I'm not sure how I feel about it. Ted Black walks in with Rocco Moretti and two women. I know that Ryker sees them because his hand tightens on my knee. They start walking to a table on the other side of the restaurant, and I realize one of the women is Nadia Hoffman, Petra's mother.

"Come on, let's get this over with," Ryker murmurs in my ear. Ryker is tense as we slide out of our booth and he tells the others where we're going. I don't get why he's worked up. Ryker doesn't necessarily respect his dad, but he doesn't have a problem with him, either. They aren't close, and from what I've seen, it almost looks like his dad abandoned Ryker, because he's never at their house in Stark. But Ryker's never said anything that makes me think it bothers him. Of course it does, though. It must. It's not the same as sending your kid to boarding school so that they can have more opportunity. Especially not when the school is where you already live.

"Dad," Ryker says just as his father is moving to sit down. Ted isn't expecting to see his son, and his initial reaction is confusion, which is a normal one. But when the next reaction comes, the one where he acts joyful to see his son, it looks fake. I can't say why, but when the two hug each other, there's tension in their shoulders. I'm nearly certain they are doing it for our benefit.

"Ryker, I wasn't expecting to see you here."

"There's a half-pipe event on Sunday," he says as way of explanation. Ted glances at me, showing that he knows there's more to it, but doesn't say anything. "I wasn't expecting to see you, either," Ryker adds.

Ted isn't a smooth guy, that much becomes clear quickly. To the others listening, it might come off like a normal exchange, but Ryker's tone sounds suspicious to me and Ted trembles a tad. I'm the only one close enough to notice, I think. He's definitely uncomfortable with Ryker here.

"I was staying at the house in Chamonix and ended up watching some of the races. Rocco and I reconnected, and it's been a long time since I've watched ski races, you know. I guess you could say it pulled me back in. I came to watch another."

The explanation feels off to me. Maybe it's Ted's tone, which sounds guilty, as if he needs an excuse to be here.

"I hear that you've met my girlfriend, Roxanne Slade," Ryker says, ignoring Ted's reason for being here. Ryker introduces me to the women at the table, Nadia Hoffman and Malin Teslow.

"Sven isn't here as well, is he?" Malin asks, her English heavily accented.

Ryker points to our table, and Sven waves. I wonder why he didn't just come over here with us. I mean, it's his mother, and she lives in Sweden so he never sees her. Was he being deferential to Ryker or something? I'm still figuring out Ryker's strange dynamic with his friends. They're his peers in age and in many other ways, yet there's a power gap that throws everything off.

Malin doesn't hesitate though, and she heads right on over to give Sven a hug and kiss in front of all our friends. It's sweet to see this side of Sven's life. I know that the Teslow family is an important one in the ski industry; Teslow bindings transformed the way we click in and out of skis, and the company also designs ski boots. But Malin Teslow is just a mom like any other, and I watch her fawn over Sven and then give a hug to Player, who she must know already. As she forces Sven to introduce his other friends, I realize that Sven was probably just being a normal teenage boy when he avoided coming over to say hi to his mom. It's Ryker who's not normal.

My attention returns to the people I'm standing with when Rocco says my name. "You probably haven't seen the new FIS list. It was just released a few minutes ago. After your performance at Chamonix, you're very close to qualifying for Nationals at the end of the month."

It takes a beat for me to comprehend what he's saying. "U.S. Nationals?" I clarify.

Rocco tilts his head. "I didn't know you had dual citizenship."

"I don't," I answer. Half of my teammates do, and maybe that's why people don't talk about Nationals as much as they did at Sugarville. "It's just, we never talked about it. I had no idea I was so close."

The goals for the season have been race by race. Up until this trip, my goal was just to get my FIS score low enough so I'd be racing with this group, Stark's top team and the most competitive FIS races in Europe aside from the Europa Cup. Now that I'm here and racing, I guess I hadn't allowed myself to think beyond the downhill race in Italy next week.

"How were Petra's points, Rocco?" Nadia asks. She hardly has an accent, though she grew up in Germany before coming to Stark for school. She then skied for the German National team and I guess lived in Germany until about eight years ago when they moved back to the states for her husband's coaching job.

"Good. They are the same as Roxie's," he says carefully.

Nadia's lips tighten, and I know immediately that this is who Petra got her overly-ambitious and mean side from. Nadia doesn't want her daughter in a tie with anyone, especially a girl like me. I can't help but remember how Petra called me white trash, and said I wasn't like *them*. Skiing royalty.

"Well, Petra will go to the German Nationals in any case. She's already been invited. Her father wants her to race for the U.S. but Americans don't respect ski racers the same way Europeans do. Here, skiing is to us what football is to Americans. Petra will have more of a future racing for Germany."

"It's nice that she has both options," I say, trying hard not to snap at this snobby woman. If I cared about Petra, I'd stick up for her and ask her mother if she's asked Petra what *she* wants. I also don't point out that she sent her daughter to Stark instead of a European ski academy. Her logic doesn't fly. She's only saying these things to sound superior.

Nadia ignores me and turns to Ryker. "Well, Mr. Black, are you joining us for this meeting? We usually just debrief you after our committee meetings but it'd be nice to have you in person since you're here."

She just called Ryker Mr. Black. And she did it in front of Theodore Black, Ryker's dad. She wasn't even joking. So awkward.

But no one else seems to think it's weird, and I remember that they've been thinking of Ryker this way for years.

"No, I won't be joining you," he declines easily. "This was just a coincidence and we stopped by to say hello. We'll be having dessert with our friends."

"I noticed Petra isn't with you. Is Aspen here? Are they together?" Nadia asks anxiously. So that's why Ryker never got a call from the Hoffmans. Petra didn't tell them what happened, or what she did.

"I'm no longer friends with your daughter, Nadia," Ryker says evenly. Nadia's head snaps back as if she suffered a physical blow.

Before she can recover, Ryker takes my hand and quickly retreats.

Malin Teslow is patting Sven on the shoulder. "Okay, Sven, I'll leave you alone now. But let's have lunch together after your training runs, okay? You can invite whomever you'd like," she adds with a big smile. She says something in Swedish, at least I assume it's Swedish, that sounds like an endearment, and Sven mumbles a response.

Yup. He's embarrassed. It's cute. Ingrid thinks so too, if the adoring way she's looking at him says anything.

"What was that about?" Chelsea asks when we sit back down.

"Stark, Inc.'s outreach committee," Ryker says.

"When you say Inc., you mean the company not the school, right?" Tyler asks, and Ryker nods. "I didn't think Rocco Moretti was involved in the business."

"Yeah, for about a decade actually. Coaching is his first job, but my mother brought him in because of his connections in Italy."

The waiter comes by to take our order for dessert and I'm amazed when we spend the next half hour talking about Stark, Inc. and its various endeavors. Brad is genuinely interested, and Ryker doesn't shut them down, giving us what feels like insider info when he tells us who's involved in what and how it's all connected. For Player, Ingrid and Sven, whose families have been part of that circle for decades, it's probably not all that interesting, but they can appreciate our curiosity.

Somehow, the conversation helps me feel like less of an outsider in the Stark world. At least I know who's who now. Before I started at Stark Springs Academy, I didn't even know that Stark, Inc. was the main thing holding everything together. It basically owns all the other businesses in the winter sports industry. Not *all* of them, but a lot.

Chelsea tries to talk us into going to a bar after dinner, but she only convinces Tyler, Player, and Brad. On the way home, we decide that Player can room with Chad, Sven's roommate, so that Sven and Ingrid can have our room and I'll stay in Ryker's room. A week sharing a hotel room with Ryker... wow. My parents wouldn't approve, but then again, they did start dating in high school and got married at twenty.

I hadn't noticed earlier that Ryker's room is a suite. I must have been pretty distracted to have missed the French doors leading to another room. Ryker walks through them and we take in the couch, the desk, and the mini kitchen. Not to mention the view of the slopes from a balcony. It's dark out now, but the chair lift lights illuminate some of the trails.

"This was the only room left? Not bad."

"And I can do work in the morning without waking you."

"We could live here forever."

There's another door out to the hallway from this side, so he can come and go to get breakfast or whatever. He wakes up early normally, but with jet lag it could be even earlier.

A part of me wants to grill Ryker about Nadia Hoffman, Rocco Moretti, and his father. They're all on a committee together with Sven's mom, and they report back to him. It's so weird. And what was up with the tension between Ryker and his dad? What did his dad mean about finally watching skiing again?

But then Ryker lifts me up and carries me back into the bedroom, throwing me on the mattress before proceeding to slowly undress me. When I'm in nothing but my underwear, he just sits back on his heels and stares at me.

"Wait a second," I argue. "I said I wanted *you* without clothes on, not me. You're still wearing all of yours." And I meant something else, too, but he hasn't even touched me.

Ryker pushes back and takes off his shirt first, and I lean up on my elbows for a better view. I've seen him shirtless at the gym before, but at his house in Stark he'd put a shirt on when we slept. I'd catch a glimpse when he changed, but now he's shirtless and the whole point is for me to look. So I do.

He unbuttons his jeans and tugs them off, revealing black boxer briefs. He kicks the pants from his feet and tugs off his socks before climbing back over me.

"Ready for bed?" he asks with a smirk.

"Are you serious?

He chuckles, and when I reach to run a hand over his stomach muscles, he grabs my hand and tugs us both to our feet.

"Let's brush our teeth, you do your face wash and lotion thing you do before bed, and then we'll get on our pajamas."

"Our pajamas?" Is he joking? We're both in nothing but underwear!

"Yeah, didn't you pack the little shorts and those crazy soft tee shirts you like to wear to bed?"

"Ryker, I'd rather we hang out in bed like this, without pajamas."

"I packed shorts and a shirt for bed just for you, Roxanne. This is what I normally sleep in," he says, gesturing to his briefs, "but I was planning on sharing a room with you, so I packed clothes I can sleep in."

I can't decide if I'm actually mad, or if this is sort of funny. As I watch our reflections brushing our teeth next to each other in the mirror, wearing nothing but underwear, I have to giggle.

"We're cute, aren't we?"

He raises an eyebrow. "Sure, Roxanne. We're cute."

I do my face wash and moisturizing while Ryker leans against the counter watching me.

"I feel like an old married couple," I grumble as I tug a shirt over my head.

But it's perfect.

We fall asleep spooning, in our pajamas.

# Chapter 16

"You know the lifts don't even open until eight, right?" I ask Ryker, opening our hotel room door. We're all dressed to hit the slopes, and we still have over an hour before the mountain opens. I woke up early, probably because my subconscious remembered Ryker's here. He was already up working in the suite.

Ryker doesn't get a chance to reply because the same door Petra came out of yesterday opens. But instead of Petra, Brad walks out. He turns to the elevators, and his head is down as he lets the door close behind him. He's staring at his feet, lost in thought I guess, and doesn't notice us until he's a foot away.

"Oh, hey guys," he says. "You're up early."

He doesn't know that we know what room he came out of already, and maybe he thinks he can ease his way into telling us what he's doing here at 6:30 in the morning. But we already know.

"That was Petra's room you just came out of, Brad." I figure we should just get right to the point.

Brad puts a hand behind his head, rubbing the back of it as he cringes. "Yeah, she was at the bar we went to last night. I know you guys aren't friends with her anymore for whatever reason, but it really was just a hook-up."

"I thought you said she was annoying and you didn't want her," I remind him of the conversation we had just last night.

He cringes again. "Yeah, I had a few too many drinks. It's not like I'm going to be friends with her now. I won't invite her to hang out with us or anything."

"It's not that," I say, angry now. He has no idea how evil that girl is. I can't believe he spent the night in her room. "She's a really bad person, Brad, okay? You don't know what she's capable of."

Brad frowns. "Is there something you haven't told me about?"

Ryker finally says something, and it's directed at me. "You never told him?"

I shake my head. We are not doing this now. We're still standing in front of the elevators and anyone could overhear us. Instead, I say, "Please tell me you were safe. The last thing we need is her claiming you got her pregnant or something."

Brad's cheeks redden and he mumbles, "It was safe." Great, Brad had sex with Petra last night, a girl he doesn't even like, while Ryker and I slept in pajamas. Not that it matters but ugh, I hate thinking of Brad and Petra together. It's disturbing on a number of levels.

We step into the elevator, and I can feel both guys looking at me. Brad probably wants to know what I'm keeping from him. And Ryker, I don't know why he's burning holes into the side of my head. I try to keep my eyes trained ahead. Brad mumbles an apology before leaving to go back to his hotel. He doesn't know what she did, and probably isn't even sure why he's apologizing, but he does it anyway.

The hotel has set up a breakfast buffet for the athletes. Ingrid told me that most places in Europe just have croissants or bread for breakfast, and the teams staying at the hotels have to arrange for something more substantial. This one has the works: eggs, bacon, hash browns, pancakes, fruit and yogurt. Ryker is quiet as we load our plates. There are only a couple others in the breakfast area, and I notice them appraising Ryker. I can't tell if they are coaches or athletes, but they seem to recognize him and are probably wondering why he's here.

When we sit at a table by a window, Ryker doesn't start eating right away.

'You were pretty upset about Brad and Petra, Roxanne." He's staring at his plate and he won't look at me.

'Yeah, aren't you?" But I think I know what's wrong here, and my stomach drops. He can't think that. Ryker's too intelligent to get jealous. No, that's dumb logic. Jealousy isn't rational, so Ryker's going to feel it whether it makes sense or not.

"Not much, no. Your reaction seemed to be about more than Petra," Ryker speaks quietly, evenly, and he finally raises his eyes to mine.

I'm seething.

"Ryker, did you forget what she's capable of? Do you think it's a coincidence she's been after him since the second we got here, and he happens to be one of my closest and oldest friends? Aren't you worried she's up to something? I know you aren't close with Brad, but I would think you would care a little for my sake. In the end, she's trying to hurt me. She's going through him to get to me."

Ryker doesn't back down though. "What could she do to him? If she's using him to hurt you, then she must think you have feelings for him. Why would she think that, Roxanne? Huh?"

Taking a deep breath, I grit out, "How would you feel about Player, Sven or Cody hooking up with Petra? Would it feel like a betrayal?"

He drops his shoulders half an inch, but it's enough. "That's not the same thing."

"No, not the same, but it would bother you. And this bothers me, all right? I'm sorry if that makes you feel insecure, but too bad."

Now he looks a little regretful. "This is probably why she did it, you know?" he remarks after a moment. "To get between us. She knew it would upset you, and maybe only because he's your friend, but still, she knew I wouldn't like seeing you upset over it."

"Yeah, you're probably right."

"Was that our first fight?" he asks.

"Are we over it? Did we make up?"

"We can't keep fighting if that's what Petra is trying to do."

"She's kind of smart, huh?"

"Nah," Ryker dismisses the idea. "She's just desperate."

I take a sip of orange juice and start digging in.

"For what it's worth," I add after a moment. "I've never been upset before about what Brad does with girls, and believe me, there have been a lot. I think that means you don't need to be jealous of him."

"Maybe," he agrees with a smile, but I don't think I have him entirely convinced.

Ryker and I split up when we hit the slopes. He heads off to explore the mountain with Player while I join my teammates and coaches to inspect the giant slalom course that was set up this morning. There will be a lot of racers training on it today, so we'll probably only get two runs in before the course gets super rutted out and they have to pull it.

I can't help but notice that Rocco's attitude toward me changed after Friday night, when he spoke to me about Ryker and Stark, Inc. As we slide along next to the course, Rocco points out aspects of the line, and he seems to make eye contact with each of the other nine on our team, except for me. It's hard to deny that he's engaging everyone else in a discussion about the course, but he's not addressing me. What's up with that? I'd hoped he'd realize how out of line he'd been and we'd just move past it, but it seems like he's actually mad at me for not getting on board with whatever he wanted.

When Rocco leads us down to the hill to inspect the course from another angle, Lia holds me back. She points out a few more things with the line Rocco just went over, and we discuss the importance of turning high when I come over the knoll.

"I'm sorry Rocco is acting this way, Roxie. Don't take it personally." She doesn't allow me to ask any questions before she slides down to join the group, leaving me more confused than ever.

The course gets super dug up with both the men and women racers running through it. But I'm learning that I ski best under adversity, whether it's the terrain or the weather, and I attack the training course on both of my runs, as if it's a race.

I'm trying not to let the possibility of going to U.S. Nationals overtake me and weigh me down. I know if I let it, I'll obsess. I still haven't even looked at my FIS points because I know how distracting it can be to focus on numbers and rankings instead of the actual course I'm racing. So far, approaching it one race at a time seems to be working, and I'm going to do my best to keep that rhythm going. Still, the idea that there's something big looming ahead of me, as long as I keep it in check, gives me a new surge of energy and makes me want to attack the course with renewed ferocity.

Lia notices, and gives her usual subdued praises, but Rocco doesn't say anything.

Ingrid snaps out of her boots beside me and looks around us as she hoists her skis on her shoulder to walk over to the ski lockers by our hotel.

"Hey, have you run into the guys from the Canadian Team?" she asks.

"I did yesterday right before Ryker got here, and I saw a few of them at breakfast this morning. But since Ryker showed up, they keep their distance."

"Oh yeah, I forgot about that. He didn't want you partying with them at Beaver Creek."

"He said he didn't want any of the Stark girls to, but yeah, pretty sure it was just me. Why? Have they been talking to you?"

Ingrid had definitely been interested in Carter Leduc when we were at the Beaver Creek Carnival, even convincing me to go to a party in his hotel suite with her. I haven't mentioned yet that he asked me about her yesterday.

"Yeah, I saw them in the elevator this morning and they invited me to a party tonight. Sven was with me and he told them the women race tomorrow so I can't go. It was embarrassing. Not that I would've gone, but I don't know."

"What's going on with you and Sven? I can see you guys are into each other, but I was a little worried Ryker was getting carried away switching around the rooms so you two had one together."

We get to the lockers and drop our skis.

Ingrid tells me that yeah, she freaked out at first about staying overnight with Sven, but it was fine. "He didn't try to do anything really. We just watched a movie and went to bed."

I give her a skeptical look and she flushes. "Well, we did some other stuff in the afternoon when you gave us the room. Just kissing. It was nice. I think he knows I don't have any experience."

"Join the club," I tell her. We leave it at that. Neither of us are the type of girl to go into detail about it. "So, what about Carter? Have you seen him? How was it left with you two?"

As we head in the back door of the hotel and hit the elevator button, I tell her that he asked about her when I ran into him yesterday.

"I saw him at the top of the course right before I did a run. We said hi, he said we're staying at the same hotel and should hang out, and then I had to go do my run."

"Don't overthink it." I try to give her some advice, because I think that's what she wants. And since I'm not sure she even knows how she feels about any of it, there's no point trying to figure it all out. "Just focus on your race tomorrow, enjoy sharing the hotel room with Sven for now, and you know, flirt with Carter if you feel like it if you run into him again. Or don't. Yeah, sorry, I'm the worst at this. I've got no clue."

At least we're both laughing when she gets out on her floor and I take the lift up to the next one. I'm not sure if Ryker is still on the mountain when I open the door into the bedroom. I'm about to call out to see if he's in the living room portion, but then I hear his father's voice, and I stop. I have the distinct impression it's a serious conversation, because they are speaking in low, tense voices, even if I can't hear the words.

I should turn around and leave, or go into the restroom and turn on the shower. I definitely shouldn't take off my boots and walk closer to the open door separating the two rooms. But I have too many unanswered questions where Theodore Black is concerned, so I sneak closer, and listen.

# Chapter 17

"Why are you doing this? Are you doing it to hurt me?" Ted asks.

Ryker's voice is clear when he answers, "Not everything I do is about you, Dad." He sounds dominant and in control, even with his father.

"You put me on the committee with Rocco to hurt me, didn't you?" Ted's voice, on the other hand, is almost trembling. I can't tell if it's because he's upset about whatever they're discussing, or if he's scared. But why would he be afraid of his own son?

"Is he the one who told you? It seems you agree on something, then." Ryker avoids answering the question.

"He spoke to me about it after dinner last night, yes. He's concerned you're making an emotional decision that you'll come to regret. After all, once you appoint a new CEO, the position is no longer yours. You can't later decide you want it back."

"I'm well aware of the consequences. But this is my decision, not yours or Rocco's."

"Is this about the girl? Roxanne is a very nice girl, and I don't have any problems with her, but she isn't trying to get you to do this, is she?"

Ryker loses some of his control at that question. "My relationship with Roxanne is not your concern. You might have a right to be concerned with Stark, Inc., since your wealth is tied to its success, but you will not bring up Roxanne again. I don't want you talking to her, either."

What? Whoa. Why?

Ryker continues, and I realize my finger nails are digging into the palms of my hands. "I know it wasn't pure coincidence that you ran into her in Chamonix and that you decided to have dinner with the team, after years not interacting with them. But I'm telling you now, you will stay away from her." There's a distinct implied threat there, but I don't know what it is.

I find myself backing away from the door slowly as my heart beats frantically in my chest. Why is Ryker threatening his father about me? As I retreat into the bathroom and gently shut the door, regret pushes down on me. I shouldn't have listened to that conversation. It wasn't for my ears, that's for sure. How am I going to pretend I didn't hear it? Should I even try, or should I just confess?

I'm still leaning on the bathroom counter, trying to figure out how to handle this, when Ryker walks inside without knocking. He isn't surprised to see me, and his turquoise eyes penetrate me.

"How much did you hear?" he asks.

My hands tighten around the edge of counter. "Enough to be really confused. I'm sorry I listened. I should have walked away or said hello so you knew I was there."

Ryker doesn't give anything away. He doesn't reassure me or tell me I'm forgiven, but he doesn't look angry either.

"I heard you come in, but I don't know when you came to hide in the bathroom," he says evenly.

"When you started telling your dad to stay away from me," I admit quietly. I don't ask him why he did that, because I don't feel like I have that right. He'll know I'm curious and he can decide how much to explain.

Ryker's leaning against the opposite wall, arms crossed, studying the floor. I have no idea what he's thinking or feeling, and it's a little scary. He threatened his own father. He told Ted to stay away from me. There's a secret out there. A big one. I just know it.

But I also know that Ryker isn't going to tell it to me. Not any time soon, and maybe not ever.

"My father was," he hesitates, looking at the floor, before saying, "not himself when my mother died. He started leaving me alone at the house in Stark for weeks, and then months, at a time."

"You were only twelve," I whisper.

Ryker looks up, but only meets my eyes for a moment before looking off. "He became a recluse, disappearing to different corners of the world under the guise of travel. We had housekeepers that my dad hired to get groceries, drive me to and from school, that kind of stuff."

"No one else knew that you were on your own?"

Ryker shrugs. "If they did, they didn't know what to do about it. My uncle suspected some of it, I think, though he didn't know how much I was alone. He would call and visit, and tried to be a part of my life, but he lives in California with his wife, and we were never very close. If my teachers or coaches tried to reach my dad, I don't know. He was hard to get a hold of, and he was still a powerful guy, or at least, people thought he might be, if he decided to use his position."

"But he didn't. He just kind of, disappeared," I fill in. "And now he's starting to come back?"

Ryker's eyes meet mine again, and I know he's hiding something. It's not that his eyes hold guilt; it's actually more like sadness and longing. As if he wants to tell me, but he can't. Or maybe I'm imagining all of it. Maybe *this* is his secret: that his father abandoned him. Except that doesn't feel right, because I already kind of knew that, if not the full extent of it. And his friends at Stark know it as well. Besides, it doesn't explain why Ted seems almost afraid of Ryker, his own son.

"He approached me when he was in Stark over Thanksgiving." I'm struck by how he phrases that: his own father, who presumably stayed at the same house, "approached" him. "He told me he felt isolated and he wanted to be involved in Stark, Inc. We had an opening on the outreach committee, and he has some experience in that area, so I put him there. He doesn't have a board position. He'll have to earn that."

I want to ask so many questions. Why did Ted think that Ryker was trying to hurt him? And why would it hurt Ted to be on the same committee as Rocco? But the biggest question burning me up is why he wants his dad to stay away from me.

"Since my mom died, my dad hasn't been watching ski races, or even skiing, as far as I know. My mother never reached world-class level, but she was a good skier, and she and my father met on their college ski team."

Ryker's giving me information, but he's censoring it, holding back. His words are delivered thoughtfully, and not emotionally. It's as if he's trying to give me as much truth as he can without telling me the most important part. I don't know what a guy who's spilled all his secrets looks like, but it's not Ryker Black. Ryker is wound tight, holding it in. But I don't know who he's protecting.

There's a long pause. We're only a couple feet away, standing in the bathroom together, but it feels like we could be miles apart. He's waiting for me to ask questions, and he's tense, figuring out how he'll answer them. I'm waiting to see if he'll tell me anything else, because I'm not going to ask questions he doesn't want to answer. Especially if it's not really my business. I was the one in the wrong, eavesdropping, even if I'm the one frustrated and maybe even a little angry. I'm not mad at Ryker, but at this secret, whatever it is, because it's creating a wedge between us.

"I'm going to take a shower," I tell him, after it's clear neither of us is going to say anything else.

He nods, resolved that we've reached a stalemate on the issue of my eavesdropping and his sharing. He knows that I know there's more, and I know he's not willing to tell me. We're just going to have to live with that.

*\*\**

The guys race first for this series, and my first race in Austria isn't until Friday, three days after we arrived. It's a bluebird day – sunny, without a cloud in the sky – and the snow is soft from warmer temperatures. Ingrid likes racing on days like this, and she hasn't stopped smiling since I saw her at breakfast this morning.

Maybe I'm weird, but I hate racing when it's sunny and nice out. There's nothing to overcome but the race itself. No visibility issues, no black ice, no frigid temperatures. It's just the gates and the ski racer. My brain goes haywire when I'm racing on days like today, overthinking my line and second-guessing my ski alignment, my position, everything.

Ryker senses my jitters when he rides up on the lift with me before my first run. "You okay, Roxanne?"

"I'd be better if there was at least a headwind or something. I hate it when the weather is perfect."

Ryker laughs. "You're serious?"

I explain to him how I seem to race best when the weather's really bad. "The snow is soft, so we'll all be slower. Slow is my enemy. It allows me too much time to think. Fast and dangerous is way better because then everyone has to rely more on instinct than brains."

Ryker watches me from under his goggles for a beat. "Are you trying to say you're not very smart?" He's not even teasing, I don't think.

"I'm smart enough. It's just that I do better when I do my thinking ahead of time when I inspect the course, pick a line, and visualize it. Then when I'm racing I can just go through the motions of what I already went over in my head. When I'm racing well, I go on feel and instinct without thinking about it. But if I overthink it, I screw it all up."

"Are you sure you didn't just decide at some point you're better at bad-weather races, and now you convinced yourself it's true?"

"No. It's always been that way." I get where he's going with that, but the thing is, I know myself as a racer, and I know what happens when I'm on the course.

"Maybe you can pretend that slow snow is actually a bad thing. A lot of racers don't like sunny days for that reason. Your skis can stick, and if you don't hit the edge just right, you can lose all your momentum on soft snow."

"You're saying I should pretend like bluebird days are the toughest race days?"

"You don't even have to pretend. They're just hard for different reasons."

"Yeah, okay, I'll try." We reach the top of the lift and hop off our chair.

Ryker gives me a kiss before he heads down a different run, and I go to the start of the race. I'm earlier than usual, but with the warm weather, I don't need to worry about getting cold.

Snapping out of my boots, I put my headphones in my ears and start my usual pre-race playlist, closing my eyes and taking myself through the course. The snow will be slow, and that does make it hard, in a different kind of way. Remembering Ryker's words, I race the course over and over again in my head, only opening my eyes to tell Ingrid good luck, and to touch base with Lia.

This race is filled with some of the top racers in the world, some from National Teams and many on the cusp of racing on the World Cup circuit. Beaver Creek and Chamonix were the most competitive races I'd been at until this one. I can't rely on the sunshine as an excuse for racing poorly. With Ryker here watching, I want to show that I haven't just been getting lucky. I'm a strong racer in all disciplines, and under all conditions.

I snap back into my skis and a moment later they call my name and number. I don't mind that I've got to keep proving myself. The best racers keep on proving themselves, over and over again, and I'm not the best, not yet. I'm still climbing up, and I won't let slow snow bring me down a step.

# Chapter 18

The first drop is a steep one. Even with slushy snow, there's an opportunity to pick up serious speed. I tuck low and put all my strength on my lower ski, carving through the turns just as I imagined in my head. I'm chanting "speed, speed, speed," over and over in my head and it's drowning out the other voices threatening to make me overthink and second-guess myself. My skis arc around one gate and slide to the other side of my body, bringing me into a perfect position so I'm turning high above the next gate, allowing time to pick up speed before rounding into the next turn.

I keep my body low, and my muscles firmly engaged, repeating the mantra louder and louder as I gain speed.

Speed.

Speed.

*Speed.*

My legs are grounded with my skis to the snow as they swerve back and forth through the course. I'm leaning forward, using my body weight to propel me down the fastest line through the gates. The snow wants to slow me down, but on the course it's packed down enough to allow me to dig in my downhill edge and fight through the resisting terrain.

When I get through the final steep section and see the flat runout ahead, I keep chanting away the voices telling me if I'll lose all my momentum if I don't hit it just right. No, I ignore the thoughts that I'm turning too early or too late, too wide or not wide enough. I just get into a full-on tuck, low to the ground and poles drawn in close to my body, and I ride it out.

The crowd at the bottom roars, and I'm unsure whether their energy is a result of the great weather and ability to view the entire course clearly, or if they're actually excited about my race.

My chest heaves up and down as I come to a stop. I'm dizzy from the exertion and my face, my whole body, feels hot. The "speed" chant takes a few seconds to die down in my head, and I pull my goggles up to try to get some clarity. I'm spinning from the rush, one I've only ever experienced racing downhill. My eyes land on Ryker, and a wide smile takes over his face, dimples and all.

I don't know how my eyes gravitated to him but I know when I see his face that I just killed it. Snapping out of my skis, I finally come out of my haze enough to hear the commentator.

"Slade's time moves her into third place, pushing everyone else back a spot. Slade has shown that any bib number has a shot at the podium. We'll have to see if she can maintain her position on the second run today."

I'm not worried about that. I think I've finally figured out how to get past the barriers holding me back. They were all in my head. My body is totally capable of racing fast in every discipline, and it's a lot more fun when I can get over those insecurities and just embrace the course.

Instead of heading straight for Rocco when I exit the race area, I go to Ryker. He doesn't hesitate lifting me up, and tells me he knew I'd rock it. Rocco tries to insert himself, telling me about the team meeting we'll have in a few minutes.

I brush him off, because that's what he's been doing to me. Besides, it's not like I don't already know about the team meeting. We have one between runs at every race.

When Ryker puts me down, I notice Sven, Player and my Vermont friends are beside him. It's a little too early for congratulations, since the second run could be a disaster, but my friends high-five me anyway. Even if I crash or miss a gate on the second run, this was another breakthrough in my racing career.

I'm running on a fresh boost of confidence and adrenaline for the second run, and it's no surprise to me, at least, when I race fast enough to maintain my podium spot. With my breakthrough slalom race in Chamonix, I knew I could conquer any discipline, but I still didn't know if I could do it in any racing conditions. Now, I feel a little bit invincible, like maybe Ryker has dusted me with a few of his superpowers.

Ingrid rocks her race as well, earning a seventh-place finish and beating Petra. With her social dethroning, Petra seems to have lost a little bit of her racing mojo as well. She's not bombing it, but she's not moving up like me and Ingrid.

When we head to the mountain the next day to watch the guys race slalom, I'm not filled with the nervous apprehension that usually gets me before my slalom races. As we watch the guys go through the tightly-lined gates, my energy spikes in a good way. I'm excited to go out there tomorrow and rip through the slalom gates, find out what kind of results I'll get with my new approach.

"So, Carter said his team is throwing a party tomorrow night after all the ski races are done," Ingrid tells me during a lull between Sven and Brad racing. "Do you want to go with me?"

Chelsea is with us too, and she claps at the idea of doing something other than sitting around, watching us race. "Yes, please! Those Canadian guys are funny. I'd totally party with them."

"Have you told Sven?" I ask.

"No, but, I don't know if things are even that serious between us. I mean, yeah we're sharing the room and acting like we're together during this trip, but what happens when we get back to Stark?"

"Do you have to know that now?" Chelsea asks. "Isn't this super new between the two of you?"

I add, "Are you sure you want to risk messing things up with him by going to a party to hang out with another guy?" I'm not sure what the answer is, but I feel like she should at least be asking herself this question.

"You guys probably wouldn't know this, but Sven had a thing for Petra all last year. They weren't a couple, because they were going to be in the posse this year and it's like, a thing, that people in the posse aren't really couples. Well, you and Ryker are, but yeah, everything's different now."

"That's dumb," Chelsea says bluntly.

"Was that a rule?" I'm just curious. I mean, he never mentioned it, but maybe that was one of the reasons he didn't know what do about us.

"Not formally, but it just never seemed to happen. Anyway, Sven was into Petra, and everyone on the ski team knew it. Then Ryker hooked up with Petra, and she stopped paying attention to Sven. I think it hit him kind of hard, and I think I might be the first girl he's been interested in since her."

"Are you saying you think you're a rebound?" Chelsea asks, while I try not to think about Ryker and Petra together.

"Yeah," she says on a long sigh.

"I don't think so," I reassure her. "I never saw anything that made me think Sven was in a funk over Petra. And you said that was last year, so it's been a long time. You haven't told us how you feel about him, though. Isn't that kind of super relevant?"

She gives me a sidelong glance. "It's definitely not a rebound for me."

I laugh. "Ingrid, I know that. You didn't have a boyfriend or anything before him, unless he was a secret."

She doesn't laugh with me. "What I mean is, I like Sven way too much. I've liked him for a really long time. I just didn't think I had a chance."

Chelsea gets right to the point, asking, "And now that you do, you might mess it up by hanging out with Carter?"

She shrugs. "Maybe I want to put it to the test, or maybe I want to hurt him first before he hurts me. Or maybe I like Carter, too."

"I had no idea you were such a drama queen, Ingrid Koller," I say, trying to lighten the mood.

The commentator announces Brad Samuel of Sugarville Academy, and we shift focus. Brad's more a speed racer like me, finishing higher in downhill and Super-G races than slalom and GS. I'm not sure if my own breakthrough with tech races recently inspired him, but he's moving up the ranks as well. Brad finishes with a smile on his face.

He chats with Coach Dillon for a few minutes and then he finds us in the crowd. We praise him on another great race, and he hangs with us until Tyler's run a few minutes later. Ever since the morning we caught Brad leaving Petra's room, things have been off between Brad and me. I didn't tell anyone else what I saw, and if Chelsea, Tyler or Player, who were with him at the bar that night, knew what happened, they didn't say anything either. Petra has no one to tell, so it hasn't come up. I still don't know if she's up to something with him, or if that was that. Maybe she just saw a cute guy who's a good ski racer, and wanted a hook-up. Extra incentive that it would get to me.

But now Brad knows I'm keeping something from him. He knows that there's more to the story with Petra, and he doesn't like being in the dark. Now that I'm in the dark with Ryker and his father's secret, I understand how Brad must feel. My secret is creating a divide between me and Brad, and I'm realizing I should just tell him what she did to me. Yes, it's embarrassing. Yes, he'll think I should tell the cops, or leave Stark, or try to save me in some way. But Brad's my friend, and in the end, what happened to me is a big deal and it changed a lot of things in my life.

As soon as my mind is made up to tell Brad, Chelsea and Tyler about what the princesses did to me, Petra shows up.

"Hi Brad. Great racing out there." She's totally using her flirty voice and it makes my stomach churn. Why does that never happen when other girls flirt with him? Is it just because I know how awful she is that I don't want her near him? Does Ryker really have a reason to be jealous?

Brad glances at her. "Thanks." And then he averts his eyes back to the ski slope.

"We've both got some free time this afternoon, if you want to hang out."

Chelsea lets out a hybrid of a cough and a laugh at Petra's blatant proposition, while Ingrid looks between all of us, eyes wide. This is all news to her.

Brad looks at me for just a second before answering. It's long enough to have all three girls wondering. "I'm going to take a nap. Maybe another time." It's not a flat-out rejection, and it makes my eyes narrow. Another time?

"You know where to find me," she says with a wink before sauntering off. A wink!

"Did she just wink at you?" Chelsea asks, before Petra is even out of hearing distance.

"Did she just ask if you wanted to hook up with her? In front of us?"

But Brad is looking at me. "Are you going to tell me what happened with her?"

Chapter 19

Instead of napping, Brad's sitting on the bed in his hotel room, listening to me rehash what the princesses pulled on me months ago. Tyler and Chelsea are in here with us too. Ryker had to work, so I didn't want to do this in our hotel suite. I get to the part where the girls drove off in their snowmobiles, leaving me alone.

"There wasn't any cell reception, so I couldn't reach anyone. It was dark and storming, so I had no sense of direction. Not that I would have known where to go anyway. We were on a mountain I'd never been to before."

All three of my friends' faces are pale. Actually, Brad's is ashen.

"I know it was stupid, and I shouldn't have gone with them. I didn't even think they were genuine about wanting to night ski with me. It was my stupid curiosity, and even stupider, I didn't tell anyone because I knew my friends, or Ryker, would tell me not to go. They had warned me already."

I tell them about how I tried following the snowmobile tracks, but they got me nowhere before they were covered up. "After a few hours, I got down to the road and walked a few miles back to campus in my ski boots. The blisters were pretty brutal, but other than serious fatigue and maybe borderline hypothermia, there wasn't any damage. Nothing permanent."

There's a long silence as I wait for them to start firing questions.

But instead of anger or outrage from my friends, Brad sounds hurt when he mutters, "I can't believe you didn't tell us this, Roxie."

Tyler and Chelsea seem to agree, or at least, they don't say anything.

"I was embarrassed that it happened. That I was so stupid. And I thought Ryker had been behind it," I admit, a lump lodging in my throat. "Monica and Ingrid had told me he was dangerous and not to defy him, so I thought when I called out the posse or whatever, this was the repercussion. It was, sort of, but not from him. The girls didn't like that I disrespected them or Ryker, I guess."

Chelsea and Tyler argue that I should have gone to the authorities at Stark or the police, which is what I expected them to say. I explain that I wanted to fight back. And again, that I thought Ryker was behind it, and he *is* the authority at Stark.

"I wanted to prove myself at Stark, show them that I could race like a badass without their support or whatever. And I did."

"So, what about Ryker?" Brad asks. "How do you know he didn't have anything to do with it?"

"I was there when he found out. I said something at the Beaver Creek Carnival in front of him and Petra and Aspen, and he was confused. I could tell he didn't know about it, especially when the girls got all weird about it. And then he made me tell him, and he was really pissed."

Brad isn't sure whether to let that go, but he keeps his mouth shut.

"So what did you do to get back at them?" Chelsea asks. When I tell them I didn't want to do anything except alienate them at Stark, my friends aren't satisfied.

I guess Ryker isn't the only one who thought the princesses deserved a more painful retaliation. "But you have to admit," I push, "it's the worst thing for girls like that. They have no status at Stark, and they won't have those connections when they graduate either."

"Yeah, I guess," Chelsea relents. "But I don't trust her now. What if she tries something again? Like, shouldn't you do something that sends a clear message and keeps her from coming back?"

Brad groans. "I really wish you'd told me all this before the other night." He's shaking his head, looking a little nauseated.

"Just don't do it again," I tell him, even though I know it's unnecessary. Brad won't be touching Petra ever again.

Tyler knows what went down with Brad and Petra, and he warns him too. "Yeah man, who knows what she's up to, right? Stay far away."

Brad's hands are clenched around the comforter. He's angry with himself for what he did, with me for not telling him, but mostly with Petra. "Roxie, don't ever keep shit like this from us again. Seriously," he pleads. "I can't handle that this happened and we had no clue. It's killing me. Even more than what I did the other night."

"Me too, Rox. I can't believe you went through all that alone," Chelsea says. "That's so messed up. Are you sure you're okay at Stark?"

Tyler gets on the train too. "You're racing well, but that place is screwed up. You don't have to prove anything, Roxie. You can come back home."

"Guys, it's okay. I'm sorry I didn't tell you, but everyone knows now. Ryker's done with those girls, and so are the others. They all have my back."

There's a knock on the door and Brad gets up to open it.

"Hey man, what's up?" Brad greets Player.

Player takes in the three of us sitting on the bed and grins. "What's going on in here and why wasn't I invited?" When none of us answer and he takes in our solemn expressions, he drops the smile.

"I told them about the princesses leaving me stranded on a mountain," I finally tell him.

"Oh, shit," he says. "You never told them? Of course you didn't. You didn't tell anyone."

"We don't know if she should go back to Stark," Chelsea declares. "Is she even safe? Your school is screwed up, Player."

"She's safe," he says confidently. "She practically runs the place now. Everyone has her back. Except for Petra, Aspen and Winter, but who cares? They won't do shit."

"How do you know that?" Chelsea challenges.

"They'll get the boot if they do. At a minimum," Player says. "And Aspen and Petra graduate in May. They'd risk their entire futures."

Player eventually gets around to telling us he's here to see if we want to go to one of the Canadian team parties. "Not you, Roxie, sorry. You still have to race tomorrow. I mean, I guess you can come, but no drinking and Ryker might not like it. I don't compete until Sunday and he doesn't care as much about how I perform anyway, so whatever."

The last time I went to one of those parties, I didn't stay for long. It was the night Ryker found out what happened. "I'll pass. You guys go though."

On my way back to my hotel, I run into Lia, who's putting her ski stuff away in the lockers nearby.

"Roxie, I'd like to speak with you," she tells me without saying hello. I've gotten used to her brusque ways.

"Sure." I lean against the locker beside her, and after she closes hers she looks around. Oh, this is a private conversation. My interest is piqued.

"I want to talk to you about Rocco," she says quietly but firmly.

I didn't think she'd elaborate on her cryptic words from the other day, but I guess I was wrong.

"Do you know why he's acting weird around me?" Does she know that he approached me about Ryker and Stark, Inc.?

"It's not just you. He knows that Ryker is planning on stepping down at Stark, Inc. and the board's going to vote on a new CEO. I know that he spoke with you about it, and that he didn't know for sure what was happening at that time. He probably hoped that you could influence Ryker to change his mind."

I scoff at the idea. "Even if I could, why would I?"

Lia lets out a shaky breath, and it might be the first time I've seen her lack composure. "Rocco isn't always logical or smart when it comes to Ryker or Stark, Inc. He's very emotionally attached."

"Okay," I say hesitantly. I don't know what she's getting at.

"As you may know, Rocco was very close with Elizabeth Stark. Elizabeth frequently spoke of her wishes to keep Stark, Inc. a family business. She thought that Ryker would make a strong leader, and, as it turned out, he was really the only capable one in the family who was interested in taking on the responsibility. His leadership skills came as a shock to a lot of people, give his youth, but Rocco was thrilled because he believed it was what Elizabeth would have wanted."

She's looking off in the distance, thinking about something else, something that she's not telling me.

"Even before Elizabeth died, Rocco was somewhat fatherly toward Ryker. He doesn't have children of his own, and through his friendship with Elizabeth, he was involved in Ryker's life. When Elizabeth passed and Ted – well, Ted struggled." She pauses, unsure how much to say about that. "Rocco wanted to continue looking out for Ryker, but Ryker wasn't interested. I think Ryker decided to look out for himself at some point, and he didn't want any adults telling him what to do."

I let out a dry chuckle, reflecting, "I don't think he needed their advice, anyway."

"Maybe not, but Rocco hasn't stopped trying to give it. Especially now, because he is worried that Ryker is making a mistake, and that he's making it because of his relationship with you."

That stings. I suspected it, maybe even knew it already, but it's hard to hear. It burns because I don't know if there's truth to it or not.

"He made this decision without me, Lia. I won't try to change his mind, even if I could, which I can't."

Lia shakes her head. "I'm not asking you to. I'm trying to explain why Rocco is struggling to treat you like his other athletes. He wants to act like a father figure in this situation, but he can't. He doesn't have that relationship with Ryker, even if he wishes he did. To be perfectly honest," she says, lowering her voice, "I think Rocco might envy your relationship with Ryker. He is a hard young man to get close with, and you seem to have accomplished it."

I think that could be a compliment, but I'm not sure. I still feel like I'm missing something. Maybe Lia is in on the big secret as well.

"So, you're telling me this to explain why Rocco can't treat me like a normal athlete? He sees me as a bad influence on the person he wants to think of as a son, but who is also his boss. I'm the girlfriend, and he wants to get in the middle of us, or use me to change Ryker's mind, but he can't, so he's just being rude."

Lia tries to hide her smirk at my comments, but I catch it.

"People don't usually second-guess Ryker's decisions, because he's proven his methods work," she says calmly. "But this one feels personal and emotional to Rocco, so yes, I think you understand. And I'm telling you because I don't want Rocco's issues to jeopardize your coaching and training experience at Stark. He will get past this, and I am here to work with you in the meantime. You are going to do big things, Roxie, and we want you to do them at Stark, with our team."

This is all too much, coming from the coach who yelled at me and made me feel like crap my first few weeks skiing with Stark. It's overwhelming me, all of it.

"Thanks."

She nods and there's an awkward moment where it feels like we should hug or something. But we don't. Lia pats my shoulder. "Get some rest. Tomorrow is another big day."

I watch her walk into the hotel and wait a few minutes before going inside myself.

Ryker is up in our room, working in the suite, and I wish I could go up there and talk to him. But I can't. There's already a wedge between us because of what I overheard, and Lia only reinforced that there's a secret out there. I should be savoring this time with Ryker, curled up together in bed, napping, like we did that first day. When we first met, it felt like there was an insurmountable gap between us, and then we managed to close it. Now, a new one is opening, and I don't even fully understand what it is, or if it means anything. If the secret is about Ryker's family and his past, why does it matter to our relationship?

The answer is right there. It matters because it's important to Ryker. Whether he's said a word about it or not, I know he's carrying a huge burden, and it's not the ones that the rest of the world sees. It's become clearer since the moment I heard that strange conversation between father and son. Ryker is the way he is for so many reasons, and I don't think I'll ever fully understand him until I know the biggest reason of all. Whatever this secret is, it's going to have to come out some day before the space between us becomes too big.

# Chapter 20

There's one thing about Ryker that hasn't been tainted by whatever he's hiding. Watching him snowboard still brings me chills. It's as if the snowboard is simply another limb on his body. He moves with such grace and confidence, zooming up the pipe and turning in the air, landing with ease. According to the guy commentating the half-pipe competition, Ryker started increasing the difficulty of his tricks this season. He's always been smooth and placed well, but now that he's adding more challenging moves to his repertoire, his overall scores are getting higher.

I didn't know all this. I knew he was good and getting better, but apparently he's about to get really big. World-class big. For snowboarding, not for his role at Stark, Inc. This one thing, it's entirely his own, without even his mother's blessing. She wanted him to be a ski racer and he learned to snowboard on his own.

It seems his decision to step down from Stark, Inc, isn't just about me. Like he said, I may have helped him make the decision, but there's a bigger picture here, and the rush of relief that comes with that realization tells me just how much I'd worried about that. But the things Ryker told me at DH weeks ago are making sense now. He's always been genuine with me. Maybe he's withholding information, but never lying.

I'm mesmerized as I watch him take his final run down the half-pipe. He's in total command of his board and his body when he flips through the air, while my heart rate skyrockets. But he lands with ease, not even taking the time to recover before catching air on the other side of the pipe. The crowd cheers at his boldness, and I am swept up with pride for this guy. He's truly amazing.

I'm still wrapped up in awe and gooey sensations about my boyfriend when he steps onto the top of the podium thirty minutes later. Player did okay, but I'm beginning to see that he's not reaching his potential. Some girls shout out obscenities at Ryker while he stands up there, and Player laughs beside me. "Man, I'm going to have to up my game out there if I want that kind of attention."

When I roll my eyes, Player slings an arm around me. "Relax, Slade, Ryker doesn't care about them."

"I know, Player," I tell him, even though it's nice to get the reassurance. The girls are a bit unnerving.

"I would totally take advantage of that situation though, and it's just going to waste with him. He doesn't even look at anyone. Basically since you showed up, it's been that way."

I'll admit that gives me immense satisfaction.

A reporter approaches Ryker when he steps off the podium, and the interview is broadcast on the loud speakers. She asks the expected questions about how he felt out there today, but then she asks him about his future.

"The winter sports community continues to be amazed by your ability to run a company and compete at such a high level snowboarding. Do you plan to continue with both these pursuits?"

Ryker's eyes search the crowd, and when he catches my eye, he answers. "I've recently decided it's time for me to focus on my snowboarding career. I'll be stepping down as the CEO for Stark, Inc. and concentrating on bringing snowboarding to the next level while finishing my senior year at Stark Springs Academy." He's looking at me while he says it, and I know the answer includes me, at least a little bit. But I'm so thankful he doesn't articulate that. The last thing I need is more people like Rocco Moretti blaming me for Ryker's decision.

The reporter is taken aback by his response. She was probably expecting a brief explanation about how he handles all of it, and instead she got a groundbreaking announcement. I don't know why Ryker chose that moment to tell the world his plans. Maybe he wanted it to be in this environment, where the focus isn't business and the people watching don't care as much about Stark, Inc. as they do about snowboarding.

Ryker's eyes move away from mine when the reporter gathers hersel11f enough to ask some follow-up questions. Player keeps glancing at me, and I know he wants to ask if I knew this was coming. He doesn't, though, and instead declares that we've definitely got to party tonight.

"This is awesome news," he says, shaking his head. "I had no idea he was going to do this."

Finally, someone who is happy about Ryker's decision. Player takes in my smile. "You knew, didn't you?"

When all I do is shrug, he says, "Of course you did."

"He didn't do it for me," I add quickly. "This was all his decision."

"Roxie, I've known Ryker since we were in seventh grade and he would sneak off to learn how to snowboard. He isn't going to let anyone else make a decision for him. But I also know he wouldn't be able to do this without you. So I hope you're in it with him for the long haul, because I know he's all in with you."

A clamp tightens around my chest at his words. There's no threat there, but I know he means what he's said, and I don't know how to respond. We haven't even been together for a month and I'm supposed to be ready to commit to the "long haul" with Ryker? I've handled being with him, so far, but I guess I'm still carrying around some fear. Fear of what exactly, I'm not sure.

When the reporter wraps up, Ryker's swarmed by people, and Player and I decide to head back to the hotel. Neither of us want to hang around waiting while Ryker has to talk to a million people. I'm feeling slightly annoyed that he didn't warn me ahead of time on his plan to announce the news today, and it makes me wonder if he did it on a whim. It's not like he knew he would win and get interviewed. That's not like Ryker though. He's a planner, not the kind of guy who flies by the seat of his pants.

Strong arms wrap around my waist and lift me into the air. "Hey!" I yell, startled.

"Where do you think you're going?" he asks as he lowers me back to my feet. Oh, playful Ryker. I like this version of him.

"How'd you get out of talking to all those people?" I ask, looking over his shoulder. Yup, there's a crowd watching us.

"I'm a talented guy," he says with a smirk.

"Yes, Ryker, that much is obvious." His light-hearted attitude is contagious, and I'm not sure I've ever seen him quite like this.

As we walk back to the hotel, laughing about how he shocked the reporter, I realize Ryker is acting his age. It seems as if a huge weight was lifted from him when he announced his decision. Whether because he's no longer keeping it under wraps, or because he's free from the responsibility his position entailed, I don't know. It's quickly becoming clear that maybe this decision is for the best. No matter how much of a prodigy he is or how much he may have thrived as a business leader, maybe he does need to step away, for now at least.

Player starts talking about the party the Canadian team is throwing tonight, and Ryker gives him a hard time, saying he would have performed better on the pipe if he hadn't been spending so much time with the Canadian team. Player isn't sure how to take it, and I can tell that Ryker doesn't usually joke about something like this. Actually, I've never heard Ryker speak to any of his friends about their athletic performances.

"Yeah, you're right," Player says sheepishly. "Seeing you up there at the top just now, it made me realize I'm going to get left in the dust if I don't make some changes."

"Up to you, man, but I don't think getting high every night is really helping you," Ryker says good-naturedly. His tone says everything. He's trying to act like a peer, like a guy on the same level as Player. He's not scolding him or telling him what to do or what not to do. Ryker's just pointing out what's already obvious, bringing it to Player's attention and letting him know that continuing the way he is won't help him on his board.

"We should still go to the party tonight," I suggest. "We're heading to Italy tomorrow."

Until yesterday, I'd assumed that Ryker and Player would head back to Stark when we went to Italy. But they don't have a competition for two more weeks, so they're coming with us and training in Italy. I'm normally not the first one to advocate going to a party, but being alone in the hotel room with Ryker is getting harder. The secret he's keeping is starting to suffocate us, I think.

"I've got a blunt rolled for tonight, but after that, I'll lay off until the season's over," Player declares.

I had no idea he was such a stoner. He doesn't smoke with our friends, which means he must do it with the snowboarding crowd.

"Do you smoke?" I find myself asking Ryker, even though it's a dumb question.

He raises his eyebrows at me in surprise. "No," he says with amusement. Of course he doesn't.

Petra's walking out of the hotel when we get there, and her eyes scan over us before she turns away. "Dude," Player says, "Brad was seriously pissed off about her when we partied the other night." Player shakes his head. "I probably should have waited for your friends to cool off after what you told them, but it was kind of awesome."

"What are you talking about?" I ask apprehensively.

"Brad trash-talked her. It was mostly dudes there, with the girls racing the next day. He said she was nuts, totally unstable. Which I guess is the truth. Brad's an even-keeled kind of guy who doesn't just spew shit, so people listened."

"The guys know Brad?" I can't help but ask.

"Some do, a little, from other races. But you can just tell right away he's not one of those big-talking dudes, trying to make drama or get attention."

Fair enough. "So, now Petra's not just an outcast at Stark?" The consequences are starting to dawn on me. And they are big.

"Yeah – I mean, she's screwed. Her image is tainted," Player says with no remorse. "I backed up Brad, and Tyler and Chelsea got on board too. The entire party was pretty much a Petra-bashing session."

My stomach drops at what that means. "You didn't tell them," I start to ask.

"No," Player says quickly, knowing where I'm going. "We didn't say shit about you or what she did."

I want to ask what they *did* say, but the elevator doors open at our floor, and Ryker pulls me to our room.

"I feel like we haven't been alone in days," he says when the door shuts behind us.

I'm surprised he doesn't want to talk about the conversation I just had with Player, but Ryker isn't in the mood to be serious. Playful Ryker is still in there, but it's overshadowed by heat.

"We sleep in this room together every night," I remind him.

"Yes, but we're sleeping."

"And now? What do you want to do now?"

He uses his mouth, but no words, to tell me. And this time, he lets me be in control. I peel his shirt off, and take my time looking, touching, exploring each inch of his chest, stomach, back and shoulders. I'm not eager to rush anything, not when I know we have all kinds of layers between us that have to be sorted through. He can't be willing to give me his body, or take mine, if he's not willing to tell me his past and share his burdens.

For now, I'll have to just take pieces of him, and I'll try not to give away too much of myself.

# Chapter 21

The party isn't in the Canadian team's hotel suites this time, but at a pub at the base of the mountain. Like France, no one checks IDs, and I guess as long as you don't look like a ten-year-old, you can order drinks. The two-story pub is overflowing with people, and many of them are gathered around the fire pits and heat lamps outside. The weather has been mild all week, and after stepping inside the pub to grab a beer, I opt for the fresh air outside. It's way too stuffy and jam-packed in there.

Ryker and I ended up taking our time in the hotel room and getting some food together, and it seems we're a little late to the party. Even though everyone's done racing, we're all in the habit of waking up early, so the festivities began early. The snowboarders add a laid-back vibe to the atmosphere; they just don't seem to take themselves as seriously as alpine ski racers, for the most part, at least. Even Ryker, with his big win today and shift in focus, is relaxed. He seems to have shed a layer today, the professional one, and judging by the way others surround him, it makes him easier to talk to and less intimidating.

We eventually get separated, with all the snowboarders asking about his competition plans and skiers wondering what his move means for Stark, Inc. I spot Brad and Sven standing around a fire pit with Chad, Henrik, Sofia and Sydney and I head in that direction. Sven sees me, but his eyes immediately dart to someone else behind me. I spin around, and Petra is right behind me. She approaches the group as if we're all buddies.

"Hi guys," she greets everyone, but no one responds. We're just waiting for her to explain what she's doing there.

She lets out a dry chuckle and moves her body close to Sven, speaking to him loud enough for all of us to hear. "Remember when you used to love any attention from me?" Her voice drags, telling us she's had too much to drink. "Now you act like you want nothing to do with me. All because of *Ryker Black*." She says his name with disgust. "But who cares what he thinks?" Petra steps up right in front of Sven, and he stands still. "Do you still want me, Sven?" she asks in what I can only describe as a seductive voice. This isn't the calculated Petra Hoffman I'm used to. No, she's drunk and trying any last-ditch effort to stir things up or get anyone on her side.

Sven clenches his jaw, and he can't really step back, with a fire behind him. "It's not because of Ryker, Petra," he bites out. "It's because of *you*. I know that's hard for you to believe, but I don't want you."

She sucks in a breath and narrows her eyes in preparation to lash out, but Sven continues with a warning, "And I wouldn't dismiss Ryker so easily. Just because he's not going to be CEO of Stark, Inc. for much longer doesn't mean he's losing power. He'll always be a leader."

It's quite the statement of loyalty but Petra dismisses it. "You're going to need to get over your hero worship one of these days, Sven. And by the way, Ingrid is inside flirting with Carter Leduc. So if you turned me down for her, it wasn't worth it."

Petra glances at Brad then. He gives her a dark look. "Are you jealous?" she asks him.

"You've asked me to sleep with you a couple of times now and I turned you down. So no, I'm not jealous. If I wanted to sleep with you again, I knew where to find you."

I have never heard Brad be so mean. Petra brings out the worst in all of us. Mean is the only way to handle her.

"Oh, Roxie got you wrapped around her finger too, does she? That's cute."

Brad opens his mouth, presumably to spew another mean comeback, but Ingrid speaks up from behind me. "How many guys have you begged to sleep with you tonight, Petra?" she asks. "Carter Leduc told me you tried with him and half his teammates. Haven't you figured it out yet?"

Petra turns slowly to face Ingrid, a girl who was afraid of her only weeks earlier. It's surprising it's taken this long for the reality to sink in for Petra, or maybe she was too stubborn to accept it. But as the color drains from Petra's face, it's as if she's finally conceding that her world, as she's known it, is gone. She's no longer the one everyone wants to be or be with. She's an outcast. And there isn't even a new girl knocking her down and filling her shoes, because the foundation she relied on has been knocked away too. Ingrid doesn't want to be the new Petra and neither do I. But we both have a lot more respect from the winter sports community than she ever did.

Petra doesn't throw out a comeback like we expect. She walks away without a word, and it looks an awful lot like giving up, but I'm not so sure.

Ryker walks over and puts an arm around me. "What was that about?" he asks.

"I think she's actually surrendering," Ingrid replies, watching Petra turn the corner back to our hotel.

"She was wasted. She might not even remember this conversation," Sven comments. "I still wouldn't trust her."

Brad adds, "I wouldn't be surprised if she knocked on my door later tonight. She did last night."

"I don't get it," I say, shaking my head. "She's not stupid. Why does she think hooking up with guys will help her get more respect or power or whatever?"

"She doesn't have much to lose," Ryker says. "And it's not a horrible plan. Guys don't always act smart when it comes to girls."

I frown at the comment, recognizing the truth to it but not liking it. If I wasn't here, he'd probably point out that Petra is gorgeous, and it's hard for a guy to say no to her. With the right guy, she could form a new group and new loyalties. After all, she's still skiing royalty. Now, though, after what Player said happened at the party the other night, it seems pretty unlikely. Of course, she probably didn't realize until just now that her demise wasn't limited to Stark Springs Academy. It's expanded beyond that.

Ingrid must have decided that Carter Leduc wasn't worth it, after all, because she sticks with Sven for the rest of the night. I know she's risking a heartbreak with him, and I'm proud of her for putting herself out there. I can't read Sven well enough to know for sure if he's falling for her, too, but I hope that whatever they have going on keeps up when we get back to Stark.

After a couple of hours outside by the fire pit, with random people stopping by to introduce themselves, it dawns on me that they aren't just here for Ryker. People want to talk to me, too. Whether it's because I'm moving up the ranks so quickly, and I'm a newbie on the European FIS circuit, or because I'm Ryker's girlfriend, I don't know. We might not have intended to end up being *those* people, the ones everyone at the party wants to hang out with, but it kind of ended up that way. Still, we're not acting all exclusive. Our other teammates are here too, and no one's acting better than anyone else.

I'm starting to yawn and lean on Ryker's shoulder, thinking about heading back to bed, when Player finally shows up. He introduces us to a girl he met who works at the outdoor skate rink a few minutes' walk away, and she's got the key to the skate rentals. Before I know it, we're all walking over there together. The entire Stark ski team, minus Petra, and most of the Sugarville team, minus Dani and Wyatt, who didn't come out tonight. Tyler and Chelsea have joined us too, and Tyler's trying to talk Chelsea out of skating. They're bickering and it makes me smile.

I'm the first one to lace up and when I step onto the ice, I catch sight of a pair of eyes on the other side of the rink, glowing in the lamplight. They disappear into the darkness, but not before I realize who it was watching us. Petra. No, she hasn't given up. And she won't forget about all of it tomorrow.

***

Italy is my favorite, and not just because we're racing downhill. It feels like spring break here, with everyone smiling and jovial like they're on vacation. We took a train down from Austria and when Ingrid and I walked through the station together, guys whistled and hollered at us. Ryker and Sven were right behind us, and I thought they'd say something, but they just smiled like it was totally normal. Ryker did come up and put his hand on my hip, explaining, "It's just like a compliment. They do it to all pretty girls. It's not an insulting thing like in the States."

It's happened a few more times, even some catcalls from the chair lift when we're inspecting the course, but no one else seems to react so I just go with it.

Ingrid's parents and younger brother are here too and it's cool to get a glimpse of her life outside Stark. Apparently Tabor, Ingrid's brother, had his final race of the year at a different resort in Austria this past weekend, and that's why they didn't make it to watch Ingrid when she raced in her home country. Geographically, Europe isn't all that different size-wise from the States. I mean, they drove to Italy in one afternoon, not all that different than driving from one state to another.

I remember the first day I met her on my way to the athletic center, and how weird it was to see a girl I knew as a racing statistic in person. Now I get to watch her pretend to be annoyed with her little brother, who keeps trying to hang out with us without his parents around. We're in full-on competing mode though, so he's stuck skiing with his parents. Not so bad, given they were both on the Austrian National Team.

Just like at Beaver Creek, we have three training days before our first downhill race. We get timed on our training runs and our bib number is based on what place we get on the training runs. For the first time in Europe, I'm ranked high enough to have a single number on my bib: eight. Though I'm proud of the number, I know I haven't put it all out there on the training runs. I held back on purpose, as most racers probably do. It takes a lot of energy, not to mention risk of crashing, when you go full force on a downhill course, and at Rocco's urging, we kept our efforts conservative.

Like Lia said he would, Rocco's coming back around. I don't know if she had a talk with him, or if he realized after Ryker's announcement that it was a done deal and that I wasn't the main reason for it anyway, but it doesn't matter. He's the main coach for downhill, and I need his insight if I'm going to race well.

After listening to Rocco hammer out advice for ten minutes, I'm relieved when my bib number is called to the start gate. I'm anxious to just go. Having raced so well in my weaker disciplines, I can look down at the gates with confidence. I own this course. It's good to have Rocco's words floating around in my head, but they aren't going to make or break it for me today. No, I'm in total attack mode as I level my poles in front of me and kick back with all my strength, levering my body off the platform and down the hill.

The weather and the terrain is irrelevant at this point. The voices in my head snap off as I crouch into a low tuck, zooming through the upper flat section in anticipation of the first steep drop off. It's a long one, but my legs don't ease off with the pressure as I dig my edges into each turn. After months at Stark, I've built a new level of strength and I'm putting it to the test right now.

I catch air on one bump after another, but there's no hesitation as I keep my weight low to the ground, centered and balanced. My upper body is in full communication with my skis, and they work together to gain maximum speed without losing stability. The jumps are here as a test, and they're sure to send a lot of skiers crashing at these speeds, but I use them to my advantage. They don't shake me, but propel me forward.

My skis and body are rattling with the speed, but I've got it under control. The final stretch comes into sight before I've even felt a burn, but maybe it's because I'm not paying attention to anything but my speed. Wind whips around me, along with my vision. I'm going too fast to see clearly, but I can make out the red gates and the course lined with blue-painted snow, and that's enough to get me down the mountain.

There's a huge run-off after crossing the finishing line, but I'm barely able to slow down before reaching the gate netting holding back the fans. As soon as the spinning around my vision clears, I hear the announcer saying that I've moved into first place by half a second. A huge lead. At that news, my legs finally realize they can stop fighting, and I collapse. It's partly from muscle exhaustion, but I'm simply overwhelmed by the announcer's revelation. First place. By half a second. It's basically a guaranteed win, and the revelation has knocked me right down to the ground.

# Chapter 22

I'm still riding the high of my win twenty-four hours later, when I slide into the starting gate for my first of two Super-G runs. Today is my last race in Europe, but not the last of my season. Rocco told me yesterday afternoon that I would definitely be racing at U.S. Nationals in downhill. I could qualify in the Super-G today, too, but I can't be bothered to worry about it. I mean, I'm going to be racing against women I've idolized for years. One race at Nationals will be plenty. I don't need another.

Still, I'll attack this course today just like I did yesterday. That's when it's the most fun. When I'm wrapped up in confidence and going after the course with absolute single-mindedness. Speed. That's all that matters.

As soon as I'm out of the gate and pushing forward through the first gate, something feels off. I'm not quite balanced or centered right. I can't nail what the feeling is, but I push it away and charge forward. My skis arc fluidly through several gates before the slope dips and I have to dig deep with my lower edge to keep from slipping. It's a sheet of ice, and I know when I hit just right, the ice can be an ally, not an enemy. When my speed picks up, I know I've carved the line perfectly for the next turn, but as my skis shift beneath me in preparation for the gate ahead, my body lurches forward.

I'm flying through the air before I realize my right ski is no longer attached to my body. I've got no time to react before my shoulder hits the ground, taking on all my body weight with the full impact of my momentum down the hill. Pain shoots through me, so hot I can't even identify where it's coming from. I'm tumbling down the mountain now, and through the haze of shock, I register that the binding popped off my ski seemingly randomly. I was shifting my body weight in anticipation of the next turn, but I was grounded, not shaky or off-balance at all.

My back hits the netting along the course, catching my weight and stopping my fall. I'm lucky my other binding popped out in the tumble. For Super-G and downhill, binding settings are usually super tight to prevent pre-release, and the risk is that they won't release when they need to in a crash, causing even worse injury. But my bindings were at their usual setting, so why did my right one release like that?

I'm lying in the netting, staring up at the white puffy clouds in the sky, and my breaths are coming and going rapidly. Still, my mind is already racing. Why? How? It all felt so unnatural and totally unexpected. After a second or a minute the same shooting pain I felt when I first hit the ground blazes through me again. Or maybe it was there this entire time and my brain was protecting me. I don't know. I've never felt pain like this before. It's splicing, teeth-gritting, and radiates from my neck across my shoulder.

I know better than to move as I wait for the medics to come get me. Something is definitely wrong, I know that much, but it's not my legs. Through the utter shock and confusion of what just happened I'm thankful for that one thing. It's not my legs. They are intact.

***

"It's a broken collarbone," I tell my friends when they pour into the hospital room after the doctor and her assistant leave. Ryker was the only one in there with me when the doctor delivered the news. Not that it was a surprise. The medics who brought me down in the sled expected as much, and that's exactly where it hurt the most.

They'd given me some pretty heavy-duty pain killers, which I guess my parents consented to somehow, or gave permission to Rocco or someone to consent to at some point. The pain's tolerable now, but still there with each breath.

Chelsea sits on the edge of my bed. "How long are you going to have to wear that thing?" She nods at the sling around my shoulder and arm.

"A month," I say, resigned.

Tyler, Brad, Player and Sven are all in the little room too. Ingrid and the other girls on my team are still racing. But Rocco is around here somewhere. I just heard him in the hallway talking to the doctor.

Everyone trades off asking me questions about what happened, the diagnosis, the recovery. It only happened an hour ago, maybe two, I'm not sure, so I'm still processing it as I try to explain. Besides Chelsea, who was in this position just two weeks ago, the guys all seem pretty bent out of shape. More worked up about what's happened than I am. It's probably the drugs, making me feel sluggish and distant and not all that heated about the reality that my season is over. Nationals is out of the question.

Ryker is quiet though, and he hasn't stopped holding my hand. He was there when the sled got to the bottom of the mountain, and he rode beside me in the ambulance, even when Rocco pointed out it should be him, as my coach. There was a brief moment when I thought I wanted my mom or dad there as comfort, but it went away with Ryker's determination to be at my side. He kept his hand in mine as the nurses spoke in Italian around me, and it kept me from losing it.

"Roxanne, you look like you can barely keep your eyes open," Ryker says gently. "She has painkillers and needs to pass out so her body can rest," he says pointedly to the crowd around my bed.

My friends take the not-so-subtle hint, giving me reassurances as they shuffle back out of the room. But as soon as they're gone, Rocco enters.

His jaw is set with determination. "Roxie," he says my name sharply but with compassion. "I'm very sorry this has happened." He's looking at me with regret and sorrow, and I know the apology is a heartfelt one, and possibly meant for more than just the crash.

I nod. "Thanks."

Rocco's eyes flick from mine to Ryker. "Have you watched the crash?" Rocco asks Ryker.

Rocco shakes his head infinitesimally. I haven't really taken a good look at Ryker since he rushed toward me in the sled, but he's definitely on edge. I've noticed that Ryker's shoulders set in a firm, tense line when he's stressed, and if something is upsetting him, the edges of his cheekbones seem sharper than usual, like he's flexing all his face muscles. It's happening now, even as he rubs his thumb calmly in circles along my palm.

Rocco takes a step forward. "What happened out there, Roxie?" he asks gently.

"I don't know," I admit. "My right ski popped off, but I was in control. At least, I thought I was."

"You were. You were hitting the line perfectly. Did your skis and boots feel okay?" he asks, frowning.

I think back to the beginning of the run on the flat section. "No." I shake my head slowly. "I'm not sure what it was, but I didn't feel totally secure. But that doesn't make sense. I tuned the skis beforehand myself. The bindings were set like they always are on race days."

"You warmed up in your practice skis or your race skis?" he asks.

"My race skis. I didn't bring my practice Super-G skis." No one did, I don't think. We already had so many pairs to bring already for each discipline. I could barely fit all of them in the one ski bag I checked.

"And you took them off when you went to the top of the course to wait for the start, I assume?"

Now I'm frowning, too. What is he getting at? Did I snap into the wrong pair of skis? No way. They were definitely my skis. They have my name written on them in permanent marker, and besides, unless I shared the same boot size as someone else, the bindings wouldn't fit. "Yeah, took them off, walked around, stretched, did my visualizing. You talked to me up there, remember?"

"Right." He rubs a weary hand over his face. "I watched the fall on the video they took, and you popped right out of that binding, Roxie. There was no reason you should have popped out of it like that. The setting wasn't right."

"But it's the same setting I always have," I protest.

Rocco's eyes move to Ryker's again before he answers. "Lia collected your skis and she took a look at them as soon as the other girls were done racing the first run," he says. "Ryker, I'd talk to you about this first, but this is about Roxie, so I'm going to tell both of you," Rocco explains. Huh? What does that mean?

"What, Rocco?" Ryker snaps. Yeah, he may have been acting all mellow for my sake, but he's on edge.

Rocco tells us what Lia told him the right ski binding was set at. "That's the setting for a beginner skier who is half your size," he adds, in case either of us were unfamiliar with its meaning. "It was set to pop out at very little impact from you. Any weight you put on the ski and you'd pop out. I'm amazed you made it that far down the course."

"That's the lowest setting you can put on that brand of bindings," Ryker murmurs. "How did that happen?"

Rocco's wringing his hands now. "That's what I was trying to get at. You said you warmed up in them, so the binding must have been adjusted between your warm-up and when you went into the starting gate. The left binding was normal."

"But I didn't touch them," I say, my head shaking back and forth. I don't doubt Lia's finding that the right binding was set so low. It explains the crash. But I don't understand how it got to that setting. "We inspected the course twice, and I didn't notice anything then. I wasn't really skiing hard though, just sliding along the course. But I did one free run with Ingrid, Sydney and Sofia, and then the four of us took the lift up together."

"And then you went right to the start and took off your skis?" Rocco asks.

"Yes. There were maybe twenty or thirty minutes up there, and for ten of them I was speaking with you."

Rocco heaves in a deep breath, holds it, and then releases it, keeping his mouth closed the entire time. "I don't like it."

"Foul play." Ryker's words come out almost like a growl, but Rocco and I hear him.

I want to deny it. No way. Who would do that and why? But the answer is right in front of me. There's one person I know is capable of hurting me. Well, three actually, but only one here in Italy. And she's even willing to put my life at risk.

"Petra," I whisper through dry lips. The pain reliever is giving me cotton mouth but my head is clear with the realization that it must have been Petra Hoffman who changed my binding.

Rocco's frown shifts from one of worry to confusion. He opens his mouth and begins to ask a question but Ryker cuts him off.

"Rocco, start asking around immediately. Talk to everyone who was up there. I don't care if the second run is about to start. I want people's memories fresh, and not mixed up with what they remember from the second run."

Rocco nods and asks, "Are you coming?"

"No, I'm staying here with Roxanne for a little while." That comes as a relief. I know Ryker probably wants to get out there and investigate what happened, but I need him here beside me right now. It's not just that I'm in a hospital in a foreign country. Or that I just learned I'll be out for the season. But now I recognize that Petra might have been behind it and it makes me feel incredibly vulnerable.

"Roxanne really needs to rest," Ryker adds.

Rocco doesn't argue. He nods and leaves, on a mission.

As soon as he's gone, the exhaustion hits me. I'm drained. Mentally. Emotionally. Physically.

Ryker takes one look at me and doesn't pry about the bindings, the crash, Petra, any of it. He stands up from his chair and I'm about to protest, ask him to stay, when he kicks off his shoes and climbs into the narrow bed next to me. Ryker pushes the button that makes the bed recline, but not all the way, because I'm supposed to be elevated. I have to stay on my back to keep my arm stable, but Ryker shifts his body to face me.

He kisses me on my cheek and then whispers, "I love you, Roxanne."

My eyes meet his and I open my mouth to respond, with what, I don't know, but he presses his finger to my lips. "Go to sleep."

"One more kiss?"

He smirks before brushing his lips along mine. I pout at the lack of passion and he chuckles. "Sleep."

"Fine," I say on a huff. I close my eyes for a minute before whispering back, "I love you too, Ryker."

# Chapter 23

I wake up when a nurse comes in to check on me. Ryker is gone.

Without me asking, she says, "He told me to tell you he'll be back in an hour and he left you a note." She speaks nearly perfect English, which is a relief. I couldn't communicate with one of the nurses who was here when I first arrived. Apparently this nurse's English is strong enough to provide fairly descriptive appreciation of Ryker's physical attributes.

"He has all girls talking," she says with a nod. "The face, the eyes," she rolls her eyes to the ceiling and makes a smacking sound with her lips, "excellent. And the shoulders. Very strong. Very very strong. But the face. The eyes. Oh, those eyes."

Another nurse walks in and says something in Italian that has both women giggling. The first one translates, "It's buttocks in English. She understands it but doesn't speak it good. She said, 'and that buttock is nice too!'"

My eyes get wider and wider as this woman who is old enough to be Ryker's mother talks about his buttock. Should I tell her that's not really what people call it?

The English-speaking nurse waggles her eyebrows at me knowingly, and I just smile and nod in agreement. "Yeah." Because really, what do you say to that?

"You have more visitors waiting to see you. Should I send them in?"

"Oh, sure." But as I wonder at who is here to see me now, my stomach clenches nervously. Petra wouldn't show up to try anything, would she? I'm not exactly able to defend myself with this sling on, but she's already done the damage, if this was her doing. And after hearing about the bindings, I have very little doubt. If she hadn't already masterminded the snowmobile incident, I wouldn't have seriously considered someone could be so cruel, but now I know better.

It's Ingrid who walks in though, and she's by herself. "Roxie, this is bullshit," are the first words out of her mouth.

So she's heard about the bindings. Her face twists in anger as she takes me in, hands on hips. "Player and Sven are out there in the hallway, monitoring your visitors," she states. "And they told me about the bindings. I know it was Petra. I can't believe that bitch," she says sharply. It's the only time I've heard her curse, and twice in about thirty seconds. "She is so done." Ingrid starts pacing around the room, wringing her hands. "If Ryker doesn't ruin her, I will."

Whoa. Remind me never to piss off Ingrid Koller. "Is that steam coming out your ears?"

Her eyes jerk to mine and she sighs with a tight smile. "Sorry. How are you holding up? I just found out and I'm not handling it well. What about you?"

"I think pain meds help with anger management. They should look into that. Like, I know I should be seething that this was probably a set-up, but I'm not. It sucks, but, I don't know."

Ingrid stops pacing and sits in the chair beside my bed. "You think maybe it's because you had such an epic season? Like, even though you can't go to U.S. Nationals now, you know you qualified at least?"

"Yeah, probably. I accomplished all my goals." And then some, actually. "This isn't a permanent injury. Crashes happen."

"Look at you, Roxie, all chilled out." She eyes me curiously. "I don't think it's just the drugs either."

"Tell me about your race," I demand, wanting to hear about something else.

Ingrid did okay, considering Super-G isn't her strongest discipline. She's qualified for Austrian Nationals in slalom and giant slalom, and knew she didn't really have a shot in the Super-G anyway. She tells me how the other girls on the team did, smirking when she informs me that Petra didn't race particularly well on either run.

She must sense I don't want to talk about myself, because she starts to talk about Sven. "He told me last night that he wants us to be serious. He doesn't want it to end when we get back to Stark."

"That's awesome, right?"

Her cheeks turn a light shade of pink. "Yeah. I'm so glad I took your advice about Carter. I might have screwed everything up, and only because I was scared Sven didn't really care about me like I did for him. But Sven made it pretty clear he didn't like the idea of me even talking to guys like Carter," she tells me with a cute little shrug.

"You mean, hot guys who might be competition to him?" I clarify.

"I guess."

"I'm happy for you guys," I tell her, genuinely.

Her eyes meet mine when she says, "I should be thanking you, you know? You got rid of the social barriers that prevented anything from happening between us." When I scoff, she shakes her head. "I'm serious. He hardly paid attention to me before, and then it's like he realized he wasn't in a fish bowl anymore. Is that the right expression?" she asks at my frown.

"I don't think so."

"I just mean that the posse was not a good thing for anyone, not even those who were in it. And if it wasn't for you, it'd still all be the same. You made a lot of lives better when you came here and challenged it. We all got used to the status quo and didn't question it. You were brave."

"Whoa, Ingrid. That's a bit much." I'm getting a big lump of emotion in my throat at her praise.

She shrugs again.

"It's going to be weird to go back, huh?" she asks.

I swallow down the lump as a new wave of emotion assaults me. I'll be at Stark, but I won't be able to ski. I won't be able to do any kind of training. What am I going to do with myself? Sit around?

"Yeah, I'm sure it'll be fine." I'm trying to reassure myself, but Ingrid gives me a funny look. Right, she was trying to talk about all the changes, and she's not worried. She's looking forward to going back, because things will be better. But as the reality of my situation sinks in, I realize I'm not looking forward to returning to Stark in a sling. No, I'm dreading it.

Ryker walks in then, and heads straight for me, not bothering to ask if he's interrupting. I like that he assumes he's welcome, because it's the truth anyway. He's still dressed in snowboarding gear, and I'm surprised he didn't take the time to change. But then I notice the expression on his face. He's not smiling and the tight pull of his mouth can only be described as grim.

"I've got a visitor who needs to tell you something." He doesn't bother with a greeting.

"Where?" I glance behind him and spot Lina Friesan, a Canadian racer who rivals Telly Valentini in size. She's a year older than me but we've been racing against each other for years, since her home mountain is only a few hours from Sugarville, across the border. "Lina? Hi." We know each other, but we're not exactly friends and certainly not the kind of friends who visit each other in hospital rooms.

"Hi, Roxie," she says with a hesitant smile as she approaches. Lina seems nervous, which makes me nervous. "I think I know why you crashed," she blurts out.

My heart rate picks up and my palms sweat. She knows? How? What does she know? Lina glances at Ryker, who's watching me. I shoot him a questioning gaze, hoping he'll understand my confusion. How much are we sharing here?

He tells Lina, "Tell Roxie what you saw."

She must have been waiting to confirm she had permission or something, because Lina stops hesitating and starts talking. "I saw Petra adjusting the binding on your skis," she says. "I mean, I think it was your skis, now that I know what happened. She was kneeling over them while you were talking to your coach, and I remember thinking it was weird. At the time, I assumed they were her own skis. Obviously, I would have said something sooner if I knew what she was doing," Lina adds quickly.

I realize that I'm leaning forward, readying myself to jump out of bed at the confirmation that it was actually Petra who did this to me. But I don't know what I think I'm going to do.

Lina continues, "I knew it was weird that she'd be adjusting her binding minutes before the race started, but it never even occurred to me that she'd be doing it to cause you to crash, Roxie."

"Did she see you watching her? She just did it out in the open like that? Was anyone else watching?" I know Petra's cruel, but I didn't take her to be that stupid.

"She saw me watching, and then she stopped. But she didn't say anything. She's never spoken to me. Petra's not known for being the friendliest," Lina adds, as if we didn't already know it. "Maybe she didn't think I'd figure it out, or maybe she thought I'd be too scared to say anything."

"Or maybe she didn't care," I murmur. Petra must have lost a few screws when she got shunned from not just Stark society but the whole ski community. She was desperate. And desperation makes people do stupid things.

"I still didn't put it together after I heard you'd crashed. I had no idea she, or anyone, could do something like that. But by the time the second run was over, everyone was talking about your crash and how suspicious it was. I found Ryker and figured he was the best person to tell about what I saw."

Ingrid is standing up now, and her face is red with anger. "Where is she, Ryker? We can't let Petra get away with this." An image of

Ingrid tackling Petra flashes through my mind, and I have the strange urge to start laughing. But I hold it together.

Sitting here on this hospital bed, with Ingrid ready to throw some punches, Lina's giant form over my bed, telling me what she witnessed, and Ryker standing by monitoring the whole thing, I can't help the hysteria threatening to bubble out of me. This is my life and it's nothing short of absurd.

No one responds to Ingrid and I realize I'm supposed to say something. All three sets of eyes are on me, expecting some sort of reaction. But Petra already shocked me once with her cruelty, and this time it doesn't hit as hard. Yes, I wasn't exactly prepared for it and it caught me off guard, but I knew she'd do something to me at some point. I knew it.

So I'm fairly calm when I thank Lina for telling us what she witnessed and tell Ryker to kick Petra out of Stark immediately. "No need to beat her up, Ingrid," I add, coolly. Is it the pain killers or is this really not hitting me as hard as it should? I'm out for the season, lost my shot at going to Nationals, and the same girl who left me stranded in a blizzard just set me up for a serious crash.

Lina and Ingrid watch me carefully before saying their goodbyes, apparently wondering why I'm not exploding in outrage at the situation.

Ryker sits on the edge of my bed, and doesn't say anything for a few minutes. Finally he asks me if I want him to fly my parents out here to be with me.

"No, that's too much," I respond immediately. "We fly back in two days anyway," I add. Back to Stark, where I'll be watching everyone else train. "Maybe I can fly back to Vermont though," I suggest as the thought occurs to me that it'd be nicer to be home and have my parents dote on me than to be holed up in my dorm room at Stark, surrounded by people doing everything I wish I could be doing.

Ryker's head snaps up at that suggestion. "What? You want to go back to Vermont?" His voice is tight with an emotion I can't identify.

"Not permanently," I say.

Ryker's eyes are narrowed, and I don't think he believes me. The space that's been growing between us suddenly seems huge. Here we are, alone in a foreign hospital room, and I've been stripped of the ability to do the one thing I love most, at least temporarily. Though Petra is definitely crazy and she's ultimately responsible, Ryker's own misguided attempts at running Stark's social world can certainly hold a piece of the blame. And I don't even care about that, not really. It's this secret I know he's carrying, and I know it's a huge piece of the Ryker Black puzzle. He's shared so much with me, I know this, but it's not enough. There's more to his story, and I'll never fully understand the man sitting on my bed if he keeps holding onto his secret.

As he continues glaring at me, I know he thinks that my suggestion to go back to Vermont holds greater significance, and maybe he's right.

# Chapter 24

An overnight stay in the hospital was probably excessive, but who am I to question an Italian doctor? After the conversation about going back to Vermont, Ryker got real quiet. He stuck around for a couple of hours, but he was distant. I didn't know it was possible we could feel something as strong as love for each other, and still have this space between us. We haven't even been a couple for very long, yet something has been developing between us since that very first day I arrived at Stark.

Despite everything, Ryker's loyalty to me is undeniable. The more he lets me in, each layer he's shown me, the deeper I fall. And even though he's holding something big back from me, I can't help it, I've already fallen for him. That might not be enough, though. Not with Ryker Black, and not in the world he lives in. We can't have something big between us when there are so many other factors already threatening our relationship.

"You aren't even watching the movie." Chelsea interrupts my thoughts and pauses the movie we're watching in my hospital bed. She's sitting beside me with a computer on her lap.

"Yeah, I'm distracted," I admit. Ryker left a couple hours earlier and I could tell he was conflicted. He wanted to stay with me, but we needed space. No, that wasn't it – the space was already there, and it was actually kind of painful being in close proximity. It's like tug-o-war between us. Leaning forward and getting closer and then pulling back. I don't know. Bad analogy. But it feels like gravity is at play here, in a metaphysical sense.

"Didn't you decide not to take the last dose of painkillers?" Chelsea asks, watching me.

"Yeah, I just had ibuprofen."

"You feel okay?"

"It hurts, but the pain reminds me to stay still, which is good, right?"

Chelsea nods but she's biting her lip. As if she can read my mind, she says, "You should come back to Vermont, Rox. We can be injured together."

I offer a weak smile. "I was thinking about flying back there for a few days so my parents could pamper me."

"I meant for the rest of the year. And maybe next year, too," she says. "I know your skiing is taking off and you've been able to go to bigger races than ever before with your scholarship, but Rox, I'm worried. I mean, look at what happened to you."

She has a point, and even though I shouldn't brush off her worry, it's instinct. "It's just one crazy girl. Petra's getting expelled and she'll be gone. Not everyone at Stark is crazy." But even to my own ears, I don't sound convincing.

"Right, that's why two of her besties helped her leave you stranded in a blizzard in the middle of the night. And why you were too scared to tell anyone." Chelsea's words hurt, but she's right. I didn't tell her at first because I knew this is what she would say, and maybe I need to hear it.

"I wasn't exactly scared," I defend myself. "I just wanted to prove I could make it on my own. But you're right, Chels. Stark is full of super intense people and it will suck to be there when I can't train with them. The entire point of being there is to train."

"You'll come back?" she asks, her eyes dancing in excitement. Seeing her enthusiasm at the idea of me returning makes my heart hurt. In a good way, I guess. Vermont is home, but not like it used to be. And my people, my closest friends and family are in Vermont, but not all of them. Even without Ryker in the equation, I've got a lot of friends at Stark now. They're new friendships, sure, but they already have deep roots, given all that we've been through. Loyalties were tested from the very beginning, and like everything at Stark, friendships are all or nothing.

"I don't know, Chels. I was planning on coming back to Vermont at one point but now..." I drift and Chelsea fills in the blank.

"Now you've got a super hot, super badass, kind of scary boyfriend."

"He's not really that scary," I protest. He is still kind of scary, sometimes.

Chelsea huffs out a sigh, and I look at her. "What?" I ask at her little pout.

"I didn't say anything."

"You think I want to stay at Stark with a broken collarbone because of Ryker, don't you?"

"I didn't say that."

"You did."

"Well, it's true, isn't it?"

"No! It's because it's Stark. It's where I go to school now. I had the opportunity to come race here because of Stark, and I've had incredible coaching. I've improved because I went to Stark, and I'm not going to give up because of some crazy girl who's leaving anyway."

"It's not giving up, Roxie. You can be successful in Vermont, too. Once you make the National Team next season you'll get all kinds of sponsorships."

She doesn't explain how I'm going to get to all the races that will help me make the National Team next season.

"Look," she says on another long sigh. "I'm just making a suggestion. I like Ingrid and Sven and Player and the others on your team. Maybe just come back for the rest of the year while you're recovering. It won't be so frustrating to sit out if you're home."

Home. That word again. Why doesn't it feel the way it used to feel? Stark isn't home either, not really, and I realize I don't know where I belong anymore.

"I'll think about it."

"We fly back tomorrow morning," she reminds me.

"I'll sleep on it, then," I promise.

But it's not a good night's sleep, and when I wake in the morning, I'm more lost than ever. My parents call and they are hysterical. We spoke yesterday, but now they've learned that a girl on my team, the *captain*, no less, set me up for the crash. They want me home. I tell them she's getting expelled, but that doesn't appease either one of them.

I'm frazzled from the conversation as I get dressed in some clothes that Chelsea brought me last night. Before I can gather myself and decide on what to do, Ingrid barges in, not even apologizing for catching me half naked.

"Chelsea says you're thinking of finishing the year out in Vermont." When Ingrid's anger is directed at me, I'm not as excited about this new fire she's got in her. Her eyes are accusing. "You can't do that, Roxie."

"I just got off the phone with my parents, Chelsea. I might not have a choice. At the very least, I need to fly home for a few days before going back to Stark. They know what happened with the crash and they're flipping out."

Ingrid crosses her arms. "If you leave Stark, you're giving Petra what she wants. She wins."

Her words hit me hard, because they are the truth. Except I argue anyway, "This isn't a competition, Ingrid. I broke my collarbone. I don't need the training facilities at Stark while I recover, and I do need my mom." As I speak, the anger grows. Is she right? Do I lose if I go home? "I'm only being reasonable here, all right? I didn't say I wouldn't come back next year."

"Next year!" She's shouting now. "You better not even be considering not coming back next year."

Player and Sven walk in then, and they join Ingrid's team. They tell me that Stark needs me. Everything only just changed, because of me, and if I leave, all hell will break loose. I'm a leader now. I can't give up. They bring it on strong, and I try to argue, but it doesn't work. When Ryker walks in, the room is hot with the energy bouncing around, but our loud voices stop talking at his presence.

He walks over to me, but that distance is still there. It makes it easier to tell him, "I'm going to fly back to Vermont for a few days." I don't promise that I'll be coming back to Stark soon, but I do tell him that my parents have demanded my presence. For now, it's the easiest explanation, even if it's not the full one.

"I'll make a call to change your flight arrangements," he murmurs, before pulling his cell phone out of his pocket and walking back out the door. No argument. Why is everyone else arguing over me except for Ryker? The answer is right smack in front of me. He doesn't want to tell me his secret. He can't beg me to stay at Stark if he's hiding something from me. Neither of us have said a thing, but we both know our relationship is at a stalemate.

My friends shut up after that. The decision is made. I'll go home to Vermont for a few days, and then... then, I'll decide. Even with the three-week hiatus from classes we just had, I can get away with a few more days. We've been doing some work, and I'm not behind. I just know that I can't figure this out right now. I'm too overwhelmed by all that's happened. With Petra. With my season. With Ryker. And now with my friends from both my worlds fighting for me. It's weird. Really weird. And my heart feels like it's being pulled in a million directions. Not to mention my parents. In a way, their concern made at least this first step easy enough. They need to see me, and I need to see them.

***

It's impossible for me to tell what Ryker is thinking, and I'm afraid to ask. After changing my flight, he sticks by my side and helps me through my first full day wearing a sling. He dresses me in one of his tee shirts for bed, since it fits better over my sling, and snuggles close to me. We don't say anything as we hold onto each other, and I can't help but wonder how it's possible to feel so close and so distant from someone at the same time. The guy who's got his arms wrapped around me has shown me his vulnerabilities and acted tender when it matters the most, but he's also one of the toughest and most intense people I've ever known. And secretive. With each bit of information he's given me, it's unraveled more questions.

It hasn't escaped me that his father left, completely disappeared after that conversation I overheard. I haven't even heard anyone bring him up since then.

"Petra's not coming back." Ryker finally breaks the silence with one of the few things we can talk about. Funny that Petra Hoffman is our safest topic of conversation at the moment. "And she's done for the season. The FIS board is going to suspend her racing license. They meet tomorrow to vote. Lina already gave her statement so it's basically a done deal. She won't be going to German Nationals."

I hadn't thought about that. It's not just Stark that she's lost. What she did was too public to be contained to Stark. And it doesn't escape me that it's a blemish on Stark's reputation. One racer sabotaging another teammate doesn't exactly look good. "How long will she be suspended? Just this season?"

"They'll probably reevaluate in the fall to decide if she should be allowed to race next season. And you might have to make a statement or speak with the board. But I didn't think you'd want to deal with that for now," he adds.

"Oh. Did they want to talk to me?"

"They thought it might help, but they don't need it. Not for this season's suspension. Lina's account, along with the video footage of your crash and Lia's assessment of the bindings, is enough. She could try to make an excuse or challenge Lina's statement, but the board acts as fact-finders, like a jury. They'll find her guilty."

He sounds confident, and I don't bother to ask where he gets his certainty from. "What about criminal charges?" It's dawning on me that if I wanted to destroy Petra's life, I could. Well, she destroyed it herself, but it's up to me how far I want to take it.

"That's up to you. The board can report it, but they won't do it without your consent."

"I don't want to turn this into a criminal matter, Ryker," I say apologetically, thinking he'll be disappointed at my decision. "I just want it to be done. I want her gone and I want to get better."

"You don't have to explain your reasons to me, Roxanne. I get it. You aren't a vengeful person, and you know that Petra is already losing everything that matters to her as it is. Besides, criminal charges would attract attention, and that wouldn't be fun for you."

I relax at that. He understands.

"You're exhausted, Roxanne," he says softly. And he's right. With everyone firing questions and giving advice since the crash, not to mention my lousy night of sleep, I'm barely holding it together. "Go to sleep. You'll be in Vermont with your parents tomorrow night, and you can rest."

He doesn't say what will happen after that, and he doesn't add that he won't be with me. But I do feel his lips brush against mine as my eyes drift closed, and it's enough comfort for now.

# Chapter 25

"I'm not impressed, Roxie," my mother tells me as she slides one more pancake onto my plate. "You usually put away at least five or six of these."

"Don't take it personally, Mom, it's the lack of exercise." Five days without training means I don't have my typical never-ending appetite.

My mom hums as she slides another stack of three pancakes onto Brad's plate. "At least you're still a bottomless pit, Bradley."

"Thanks, Joanne." Brad pours an excessive amount of syrup on his pancakes before handing the jug to me.

"Don't eat all of them, Brad. Tyler and Chelsea are coming by."

Just as I say it, the couple walks in the side door. They greet my mom with hugs before taking seats at our little kitchen table.

"Livy's got a thing for your boyfriend," is the first thing out of Chelsea's mouth. Livy is Chelsea's youngest sister. Thirteen now, I think. While Chelsea's parents and her other sister are avid skiers, Livy decided a couple of years ago she wanted to snowboard.

"How does she even know about him?" It's probably a stupid question, but I'm curious.

"She follows all the snowboarding social media and she's got a subscription to *Ride Times*, the snowboarding magazine."

My mother puts two plates of pancakes in front of Tyler and Chelsea. "What does that have to do with it?" my mom asks. "You told me he was a snowboarder, but is he famous? I've never heard of him."

My mom hasn't heard of any snowboarders, besides Livy Radner, but I don't point that out.

"He's famous. Not so much for snowboarding yet. But he's getting famouser." Chelsea dumps that information as she butters her pancakes.

My mom gives me a look that says, "Explain this."

Sighing, I tell her that Ryker was CEO of a company called Stark, Inc. Hey eyebrows shoot up, and I know it's not just because of the CEO part. She's heard of Stark, Inc. And there's that part about me getting a scholarship to Stark Springs Academy, which is unofficially affiliated with the company.

"You didn't think to tell me this when you told me you had your first boyfriend?"

My friends snicker but I'm not embarrassed. They know me and Joanne Slade too well for me to feel uncomfortable having this conversation in front of them.

"I was easing into it," I protest.

"Wait until I tell your father. He's not going to like it. And he's definitely going to want to meet this young man before we let you go back there. Or at least chat with him over the phone."

I don't bother to ask why this changes anything. My parents aren't always rational. My dad's going to think that Ryker's power somehow means he needs to assert his fatherly authority more heavily. Ryker isn't any old teenage boy.

"Fine, whatever," I grumble, unsure whether that conversation will even need to happen. I've been away from Ryker and the Stark world for almost a week, and I'm just as uncertain as ever about my relationship with him and my future at Stark.

"I'm calling Bill right now." My mom grabs her cell phone off the counter before shuffling out of the kitchen. "Finish those pancakes, kids!" she calls, already halfway up the stairs.

Tyler asks, "She thinks you're going back to Stark. I thought you were going to finish out the year here before deciding whether to go back next year."

Chelsea and Brad share Tyler's slightly accusatory look.

"I haven't decided. Look, it's been awesome being home, but…" I hesitate, unsure how to explain it. "I have a life at Stark now. It's not so easy to just leave all of a sudden."

It's true that I've enjoyed lounging around the house and spending time with my parents and friends, seeing familiar faces around town when I run errands or stop by the general store my parents own. But it feels temporary. Like I'm visiting. I don't feel drawn to stay, and the idea of not returning to Stark, well, it makes me feel super sad just thinking about it.

"Is this about Ryker or about Stark?" Brad asks. I'm surprised he's the one to ask the question.

"Both," I admit. But I don't want to get into it, particularly because things with Ryker and I are… complicated. We've hit a roadblock of sorts. A giant one. "What were you saying about Livy?" I try for a subject change. "Has Ryker been on social media a lot recently for snowboarding?"

"Oh yeah, they've been talking about that little announcement he made after his win in Italy last week. And he had a big interview with *Ride Times* yesterday. He didn't tell you?"

I shake my head. We haven't been talking on the phone much. Only once, actually, since I got to Vermont. And a few texts.

Chelsea shrugs. "It's probably not that big of a deal to him, but pieces of the interview are up on the internet and the whole thing's coming out in print in a few days, I guess."

Tyler adds, "Livy doesn't know he's your boyfriend. You might not want to tell her."

Girls who've never met Ryker have crushes on him? This is… weird. I'm sure not everyone follows snowboarding like Livy Radner, who's already on the track to success, but still.

"Yeah, don't want to break my little sis's heart," Chelsea says with a laugh. "Or get your car keyed," she adds, cracking herself up.

"I don't have a car, Chels," I remind her, though I know that's not the point.

"Yeah, she probably wouldn't key Joanne's Honda. Livy's a diva but she's not a total idiot."

Brad stands up to get more pancakes, asking, "You know that snowboarding Nationals will be televised today, right? You watching?"

"Yeah, I'm watching. It's not like I'll be skiing."

Tyler and Brad both qualified for Nationals. They're headed to the mountain for training as soon as they finish breakfast.

"You should come over and watch with Livy and her teammates," Chelsea says, and I can't decide if she's kidding or not. And I can't decide whether I'm curious enough about Ryker's fangirls to do it. I do kind of want to know his level of famousness amongst normal people. Livy and her friends might be competitive snowboarders, but they aren't in the big leagues, at least not yet. And wait, where do I stand in all this? Half in the Stark world, half out? If I go back to Stark, with no chance of training or skiing for the rest of the school year, what does that say? I wouldn't be going back for the reasons I originally took the scholarship and hopped on the plane. I'd be going because I'm a Stark student. Not just a Stark athlete. And because I have important relationships there, even if they aren't perfect ones. Even if I'm not about to start calling Stark Springs "home."

"Roxie? Where'd you go?" Chelsea nudges me with her shoulder. "Snowboarding Nationals? Want to watch them at my place this afternoon?"

"Yeah, sure," I agree. Why not? She's got a huge television.

Brad and Tyler don't bug me anymore about whether or when I'm going back to Stark. They know it's got to be my decision, and they've already told me where they stand. Like Chelsea, they've said they're worried about me. Sure, Petra will be gone, but after all the shit that's happened to me this year while I've been away, I get why they don't have the same enthusiasm they did when I first got accepted and given the scholarship. Back then, it was all about me pursuing my dreams and all that. Now? I don't even know anymore.

***

I shouldn't have watched the competition at the Radners' house. Chelsea didn't tell me that Livy had half the snowboarding team over, guys and girls. They knew everyone who was competing, including Aspen Davies and a couple of other Stark athletes I didn't know very well. Livy's friends were twelve and thirteen years old, and their lives revolved around snowboarding, Instagram and Twitter.

Nationals spanned several days, and I'd been keeping up with Ryker's results. He'd done well in the Big Air yesterday, and slopestyle the day before that, but hadn't hit the podium. Livy and the three other girls who were there cheered for him when we watched him on the half-pipe, and gushed when he hit third place. The boys who were watching with us weren't quite as enthralled by him as the girls, but still seemed to be rooting for him.

Chelsea found the entire thing hilarious, but she didn't mention that the guy they were watching on the big screen was my boyfriend. Sure, they knew I went to Stark and asked a few questions about whether I knew anyone on the snowboarding team, but I stayed evasive. I was so not ready to handle their reactions if they knew the truth.

I shot Ryker a congratulatory text message while I watched him stand on the podium, but never heard back. Accepting that Ryker was a big deal even outside of his roles at Stark, and for snowboarding alone, I spent the rest of the night searching him on social media sites. He had accounts, but didn't use them very much. Others, however, posted about him, especially in the last week, with his win in Italy, the announcement, and now Nationals.

It left me exhausted, and, if it was even possible, more confused. Home in my own bed, with my parents taking care of me, I couldn't ignore the loneliness that wrapped around me as I set aside my laptop and pulled the covers over my body. No texts back from Ryker, and I knew it wasn't hard to type out a few words, no matter how busy he was. Strangers knew all kinds of things about Ryker the snowboarder, but how many people really knew Ryker Black like I did? And how well did I really know him? What was he keeping from me?

My dad's waiting for me at the breakfast table the next morning.

"Mom tells me your boyfriend is a hot-shot CEO," he says, before I've even poured my coffee.

"Not anymore. He's stepping down," I clarify. "But yeah, he's a big deal in the winter sports community."

"I want to talk to this guy. He doesn't have any competitions in Vermont coming up, does he?"

"No, snowboarding Nationals just ended yesterday. His season is over."

"Want some eggs? Your mother went to a Zumba class," he explains, as if he has to apologize for why I don't have a hot breakfast waiting for me.

"Toast is fine, Dad, thanks." I pop a couple pieces of bread in the toaster.

"Well, I'd like to speak to this Ryker Black on the phone before you go back."

"I don't know if I'm going back, Dad. I might just finish the school year here. I haven't decided."

My dad narrows his eyes at me. "Why would you do that?"

I point to my sling. "There's this little game-changer here, Dad, and it's called my collarbone. I broke it on a Super-G course in Italy last week. Because my team *captain* messed with my binding." I'm being a little snarky, but I haven't had coffee yet. He knows better than to hit me with big questions first thing.

"But she got expelled, right?"

By my boyfriend, for all intents and purposes. But I can't explain that to my dad. "That's not why I wouldn't go back. It's because I'm not going to be doing anything but rehab and light training through the end of the school year anyway. I can do that here, without the Moretti siblings coaching me."

"But what about your scholarship? Won't you lose it for next year if you bail now?"

I hadn't really thought about that, now that I know Ryker is in charge. Things don't work normally at Stark, but I can't explain that to my dad. There are a lot of things I can't explain to him. When my parents asked me why Petra set me up for a crash, I told them she's crazy, that she used to "date" Ryker and was jealous of me for that and for how well I was racing. They bought it, and really, it was mostly the truth.

Why is my dad pushing for me to go back when my Vermont friends are worried about me? Shouldn't my dad be worried? Granted, he doesn't know about the other stuff that happened to me, but still, he usually errs on the side of overprotective.

"I don't think I'd lose my scholarship, Dad. They would understand."

"I still want to talk to this Ryker guy," my dad says just as the side door opens and my mother walks in.

"You can talk to him right now, Bill. We pulled into the driveway at the same time."

Ryker Black is standing behind my mother. Smiling at me.

# Chapter 26

I know my mouth is hanging open but I can't bring myself to shut it and say something. Whether it's because it's been a full week since I've seen him, or simply because here he is in my little kitchen, with my parents, but Ryker's beauty hits me just like it did the very first time I saw him. It's not that I'd become immune or anything, but something about having him here after all that we've been through and all the confusing thoughts running through my head, it's like seeing him through a new lens. Yesterday I watched him on a television screen. And now here he is, piercing me with those turquoise eyes, the color so vivid it's almost unreal.

My dad's the first one to break the silence. "I'm Bill Slade, Roxanne's father," he introduces himself, putting his hand out for a shake.

"Ryker Black, your daughter's boyfriend," he says easily. The usual intimidation factor that comes with meeting Ryker isn't present. "I'm sorry to pop in unannounced, but I wanted to surprise Roxanne."

"Not a problem. How did you get in so early? Where were you flying from?"

"I got a red-eye flight last night into New York and took a little plane from there, and then rented a car to drive from the airport."

I still haven't said anything, and I should be throwing my arms around him like I did when he showed up in Austria. But it's different having him show up here in my hometown with my parents hovering. Apparently the guy really likes to catch me off guard.

Ryker walks over to me and gives me a little kiss on the cheek. "Hi," he whispers. He won't let me stand here stupidly for long, and his little gesture helps break the ice.

"Hi," I say back.

My mom bustles around us, asking if Ryker wants coffee or breakfast, and she insists on cooking him something against his protests. "You've been traveling all night. You must be exhausted. I'll whip up a breakfast casserole and maybe some muffins too. Do you have any allergies?"

Ryker shakes his head, smiling in amusement. My mother is babying Ryker Black, and he seems to be eating it up. I can't decide whether this situation is amazing or embarrassing. Both, I guess.

"Hey, Mom, take your time. I'm going to take Ryker upstairs for a few minutes." I start to lead him away but my dad stands in front of us with his hands on his hips.

"To your room?" he asks pointedly.

"Yes, Dad. Brad and Tyler go up there all the time. Relax." Not to mention I've been at boarding school and traveling around Europe parentless. If my dad only knew that the rules in the Stark Springs Academy handbook were not the real rules.

"Keep the door open," he says gruffly before standing aside to let us pass.

"Of course, Mr. Slade," Ryker says diplomatically, and it makes me want to crack up.

"Bill's fine," my dad replies.

I make it up the stairs and into my tiny bedroom before I start laughing. Ryker watches me, his lips twitching. "What's so funny?" he asks, even though he seems to get it.

"You. Here. At my house with Bill and Joanne. I don't know. It's weird."

"Good weird or bad weird?"

I shrug. "I like it."

Ryker is careful to make sure the door remains open before he sits down in my desk chair while I sit on my bed.

"I'm not here to beg you to come back to Stark," he says carefully, before I can even open my mouth to start firing questions his way. His words bring a sting of disappointment. It seems everyone else has an opinion on the matter, and shouldn't he have the strongest one of all?

"Well, not exactly," he rephrases, looking down at the ground. "I'm here because I have to tell you a story. And it's a long one."

My stomach flutters at that, because I think I know exactly where he's going. And if I'm right, he knows that the story could change everything between us.

"I'm listening."

"Three days before my mom died, I found out she was having an affair with Rocco Moretti."

Ryker is watching my face for a reaction, and he gets one. Yes, it's shocking hearing those words out of his mouth, but the thought must have crossed somewhere deep in my subconscious after my strange conversation with Lia Moretti, because I'm not totally caught off guard.

"How did you find out?"

"I heard the two of them talking at the athletic center. It was this time of year, actually, and most people were at the mountain. I was coming back to drop off a snowboard I'd been borrowing from the equipment room, and they were in there together."

Ryker's parents had wanted him to be an alpine ski racer, like so many in his family had been. He learned to snowboard behind their backs. "Wait, you walked in on them *together* together?"

Ryker actually chuckles. "That idea shocks you more than the affair itself, huh?"

I shudder. "I can't imagine walking in on either of my parents having an affair." Yuck. Just yuck.

"No, they were only talking. And I eavesdropped."

"What did you hear?"

"My mom was telling Rocco that my dad was suspicious. Apparently Rocco and my mom had an affair thirteen years earlier and it had either started back up again or never really stopped."

"Wait, thirteen years earlier?" The timing isn't lost on me, especially with what Lia said about Rocco's "fatherly" feelings toward Ryker.

Ryker eyes me shrewdly, knowing what I'm thinking. "My dad knew about the affair and had a paternity test. Ted Black is my biological father. But Rocco wants to be." His voice is cold. He isn't particularly fond of either man, as far as I can tell. A paternity test to determine his father? An ice queen for a mother? Yeah, that would make anyone a little hard.

"Oh," is all that I can think to say. I've never felt as grateful for my steady, loving parents as I do right now. They can embarrass me as much as they want. I'll never roll my eyes at them again.

"My mom had just put Rocco on the Stark, Inc. board, and while it did have a justifiable business purpose, it was not only a stupid thing to do, given her history with the man, but inconsiderate to my father. She'd never given my dad much authority in the company, and I still don't know if that was of his own choosing or not."

"So your dad got suspicious because your mom appointed the guy she had an affair with thirteen years earlier to the board of her company? And he was right to be suspicious, I take it?" I knew the secret was a big one, but I don't think this was what I was expecting. And there has to be more. It still doesn't explain Ryker's relationship with his dad.

"Yes. Rocco was trying to convince my mom to leave my dad. He told her that even though he wasn't my biological father, he wanted to be, and he tried to tell her he'd be a better dad to me than my own father. He might have been right, but my mom didn't care about that." Ryker keeps a detached, even tone as he says it, but there's no way he can't hold bitterness about his mother's lack of love for him. It seems the woman wasn't a total emotional icicle, given her drama-ridden love life.

My dad calls up the stairs that breakfast will be ready in ten minutes, and I'm about to stand up to tell him we need more time, but Ryker calls back first, "Thanks, Bill."

Despite this heavy conversation, having Ryker here in my house is still oddly amusing to me. His powerful aura is usually a little overwhelming, and I don't know if he's even capable of toning it down, but he seems to be trying to get on my parents' good side, and it's adorable. He's still got a commanding presence, but he's being extra respectful.

"I walked away before I heard the rest of the conversation, because I sensed they were about to walk out, and didn't want them to know I'd heard. I was only twelve, and I didn't know what to make of it."

He must have been scared, and hurt. Or maybe not. From what little he's said, he never had normal relationships with his parents. Not even before he overheard all that. He grew up fast, not just because of his mother's death and his father's abandonment right after, but because of many other factors, I'm realizing. Before that even happened, he lived with the pressure to be a world-class skier and fill his mom's role as CEO of Stark, Inc.

"Should we go downstairs?" Ryker asks.

"No, keep going." He's finally talking, and I know there's got to be more.

He doesn't hesitate. "The next day, my mom got sick. Flu-like symptoms. She was throwing up and dizzy and out of it. I was never particularly close with her, and I only remember that she stayed up in her room. She'd never been one to let anything keep her from working, so I knew it was pretty bad. My housekeeper took her to the hospital the next morning, and she died a few hours later."

"Wow. I didn't think you could actually die from the flu. I mean, I know infants and really old people can, but your mom was what, forty-something?"

"Forty-three."

"I'm sorry, Ryker. I had no idea about the circumstances. It came so suddenly, and after you discovered the affair. I can't even imagine." And then his dad broke down emotionally and abandoned him. But that still doesn't explain why Ted Black seems frightened by his own son, or why Ryker warned his dad to stay away from me. What am I missing?

Ryker stands up and walks over to my window, not reacting to my words. "I was immediately suspicious of my father, after what I had heard just days earlier."

That makes the hair on my skin stand on end. Seriously? That was his reaction to his mom's death? I'm basically a detached party here, listening to him retell something that happened years ago, and even I didn't think to be suspicious of Ted. "You mean, you think your dad might have…" My voice drifts. I can't bring myself to say it.

Ryker's still looking out the window when he drops the bomb. "I'm nearly positive my father murdered my mother." He turns his eyes to me and says quietly, "He poisoned her."

# Chapter 27

"He... what?" Did Ryker just tell me his father murdered his mother?

"He used ethylene glycol antifreeze. It's the main ingredient in engine coolant, or antifreeze. I saw a documentary about wives poisoning their husbands with it a few months after my mother died, and it clicked."

"But, how do you know? Did you tell anyone? Wouldn't the doctors have been suspicious?" This can't be right. Ryker's a business prodigy, not a conspiracy theorist. He's rational and logical, not a lunatic. He saw a documentary and reached this conclusion? If this is the secret he's been holding onto, I don't want to belittle him. It's obviously something he really believes. But I can't just sit here and believe him either. This is too far-fetched.

"Like I said, I was immediately suspicious. I didn't think my dad had any kind of backbone, particularly when it came to my mother, but I knew how much he worshipped her. He idolized the woman, so much so that he was a crappy father even before she died." Again, Ryker doesn't sound bitter about it, just practical. It's unnerving that he seems to be at peace with his parents' neglect. "He was either too wrapped up in my mother to focus on me, or she instructed him not to be too nurturing. As if too much love could have hurt me. Who knows?"

"But if he was so obsessed with her, why do you think he would kill her?"

"Because he found out about the affair. He already took her back once, years ago, after the affair first started, and the second time it happened, or when he found out it was still happening, he snapped. If he couldn't have her to himself, no one could have her. He didn't want to share her."

"What about Rocco?"

"What about him? Could it have been him who poisoned her?"

"No, was Rocco suspicious?"

"Yes. He asked me a lot of questions about her illness, and I knew he didn't believe she'd died from the flu. But there was no autopsy or toxicology report or any of that. My dad left on a flight to Europe the same morning she started showing symptoms, and I don't even think she called him to tell him what was going on. He probably poisoned her the night before or that morning."

"Why was he going to Europe?"

"He was on the FIS board back then and was still involved with the World Cup racing circuit. It wasn't unusual."

"Nobody else was suspicious?"

"Nobody knew about the affair except for Rocco and me."

"I think Lia knew," I say, thinking back to my conversation with her.

Ryker doesn't seem surprised by the news. "Lia didn't start coaching at Stark until right after my mother's death. It's possible Rocco confided in her about the affair, or that she knew about the first affair twelve years earlier, which probably happened over in Europe, since Rocco hadn't started coaching at Stark yet. Still, if she ever suspected anything off about my mother's death, she never gave me any indication. I don't think anyone else ever suspected my father except for Rocco and myself."

"And now you're telling me."

"Yes," he says with conviction. "I'm telling you."

The gravity of it hits me. Why is he telling me?

Ryker keeps going. "I know it all sounds like a soap opera. But I watched my father closely, and I'm as certain as I can be without the toxicology report in front of me. I haven't confronted him directly, not exactly, but I've said enough on the matter and gauged his reaction. He is responsible for my mother's death. And he knows that I know."

"You never told anyone? The police?"

"No. It'd be very difficult to prove at this point, and I don't want the media circus. My dad has to live with what he did and this is enough. I don't need to see him behind bars. He's not dangerous. Not unless he finds someone new to idolize and history repeats itself. But I keep tabs on him, and he keeps to himself."

"Until recently," I point out.

Ryker comes over to sit beside me, but maintains a little space between us. Whether it's out of respect to my parents downstairs, or because he's still unsure where we stand, I don't know.

"I told you he approached me about getting involved in the company again."

"Over Thanksgiving."

"Yes. I put him on the committee with Rocco as a punishment of sorts. He'll have to look at the man who had an affair with his wife. And also because I know that Rocco will keep an eye on him."

"You and Rocco never discussed it?" I ask.

"I was thirteen when I saw the documentary, and I was still on the alpine ski team. I told Rocco he should watch the documentary, that he'd find it interesting. He told me he already had. We've had some cryptic conversations about it, but never actually said the words. This is the first time I've said it."

It's the first time he said out loud that his father murdered his mother. And it was in front of me. In my bedroom. With my parents downstairs.

I want to ask why now? Why me? I know there's been something happening between us, pulling us together, even against our will, since the moment we met. Maybe even before that, for Ryker, since he saw me race over a year ago and decided to give me the scholarship. But we've only been an actual real couple for a month. I guess that doesn't matter.

"Kids!" my dad hollers up to us, and I smile at his word choice. "Food's ready!"

"Coming!" I call back.

I get up and stand in front of Ryker, who stays seated on my bed. His hands go to my hips and he breathes in deeply, leaning his head against my chest.

He doesn't need to tell me that I now know everything important there is to know about him. That he told me all of this because he can't even help it. Having a secret between us that big was unbearable, and he trusts me enough to share in carrying the burden with him. Holding onto something so monumental with him. I get it. His telling me this was even bigger than him telling me he loved me the other day in my hospital bed. He knows that even if I walk away, I would never tell anyone what he's shared with me. But he needs to know I'm not going to walk away. How could I?

"When's our flight back to Stark?" I ask.

He looks up at me then, and I see the exhaustion on his face for the first time. He just spent three days competing at Nationals and then flew through the night to get to me. But through his bleary eyes he smiles.

"Let's hang out with Joanne and Bill for one day and we'll fly back tomorrow. You can't miss any more classes," he adds.

Classes. Right. I'd nearly forgotten all about that part of school.

*** 

Two weeks back at Stark, and I can't believe I even considered waiting until the start of next school year to return. This is not the same campus I stepped foot on nearly eight months ago. The rules here have changed, and so have the people. Ryker Black isn't the same guy he was when he walked into my dorm room and told me who was boss. Ingrid has unleashed a whole new feisty side of herself. Monica isn't scared to breathe around the former posse members. And that's just the start of it. Maybe I've changed too. I'm still uncomfortable with people assuming I've got any power over them, and I'm trying to diffuse that notion.

It's the first super warm day of spring. There's still snow around, but most people are wearing shorts, myself included, and Ryker, I note, when I see him jogging across the quad in my direction. We're between classes, and he's got a backpack full of books, but it's not slowing him down.

He's grinning when he reaches me and he holds out his cell phone. "You've got a call."

"Why didn't they call my phone?" I ask skeptically as I take his.

"He didn't have your number."

I put the phone to my ear. "Hello?"

"Roxie? It's Dale Hoffman. How's that collarbone healing?"

"Oh, um, good." Coach Hoffman is calling to ask about my collarbone?

"We missed you at Nationals this weekend, Roxie, and I wanted to personally apologize for what my daughter did. I'm ashamed of Petra's actions, and I've made that clear to her."

Oh man, this is awkward. "You don't have to apologize, Coach Hoffman. Petra's responsible for what she did. Not you."

"I know that. And it's not why I'm making a personal invitation for you to join the National C Team next year. I'm doing it because you deserve to be on the team based on your racing accomplishments this season."

Did I hear that right? "Wait, I can't be on the Team if I didn't go to Nationals. I haven't qualified."

"You can. Athletes can always be personally invited, particularly in situations like yours. You were in position to make the C team. You might have only made the development team and you might have even made the B team, depending on how you raced, but you didn't get the chance." The development team is kind of like the "D" team but you have to be under age twenty-one to be on it. And "D" on *the Team* isn't anything like getting a D for a grade. It's a huge honor.

"I don't know what to say. Thank you doesn't sound like enough," I admit, unsure if this is really happening. I'm facing away from Ryker because his presence is too distracting, and it's taking all my self-control not to spin around and break into dance.

"The coaches discussed the team selections just this morning and it won't be announced for a couple of hours. I wanted to explain our decision, and make sure you had some encouragement going into next season as you recover from your injury."

All I can say is "Thank you," again.

When we end the phone call, I stand there digesting the conversation, making sure I didn't imagine it. Ryker comes up behind me and puts his arms around me. "Congrats, Roxanne," he whispers. "You earned it."

"You didn't make him do it?" I hate that I have to ask and my throat tightens at the possibility that Ryker could have demanded this.

"No. He called me right after the meeting to tell me. To be honest, it didn't even occur to me that this might happen. They almost never make exceptions like this. The personal invitation rule is usually only used for racers who've been on the team for years but have to miss Nationals for one reason or another. I've never seen it used for a new team member before. But you impressed the hell out of everyone this season. You'd been under the radar for so long, and now I'm not the only one who knows how talented you are."

I turn in his arms and pull his head down to me. His lips meet mine, and I stand on my tiptoes to get as close as possible. When we pull apart, I'm overcome with a ridiculous amount of happiness, but that doesn't mean I'm expecting a tear to fall down my cheek. I had no idea happy tears were a real thing.

"Is this for real? My life right now? You. Making the team. All of it. It's too much."

"It's real. It's definitely real," he whispers before leaning down to kiss me again.

There's a loud shout from across the quad. "Hey!" Player calls out. "Lovebirds. Classes are starting!"

Oh yeah, classes. Okay, so that helps bring me back to reality. Kind of. We ignore him and keep right on kissing.

I'm pressed close enough to Ryker's body that I feel his phone vibrating in his pocket before we hear the ringing. He heaves a sigh, but I tell him to answer it. Maybe it's Coach Hoffman with a follow-up message about my new spot on *the* Team.

When a deep frown forms between Ryker's eyebrows as soon as he answers, a chill sweeps through my body. As the person on the other end speaks, Ryker's body tightens beneath my hands, which remain resting on his lower back.

"Thank you for informing me," he says quietly. And then, "Please email me the report as soon as possible."

When he puts the phone down, the celebratory air that surrounded us a moment earlier has vanished.

I find my voice to ask, "What was it?"

He blinks a few times before his eyes fully connect with mine. "Petra Hoffman just died in her mother's hometown."

"She... what?" *What?!*

"Petra's dead."

Follow me on social media or join my email list to find out when *Black Ice*, the third book in the Stark Springs Academy series, will be released!

Find me online at:

www.alideanfiction.com

www.facebook.com/alideanfiction

www.twitter.com/alideanfiction

www.goodreads.com/author/show/7237069.Ali_Dean

Want to be one of the first to read my books?

Sign up for the ARC list here: http://eepurl.com/bJ2G4T.

Want to hear about any sales, updates, or news I have?

Sign up for my mailing list here: http://eepurl.com/bJ-okv

Ali Dean is also the author of the Pepper Jones series:

*Pepped Up* (Pepper Jones #1): http://amzn.to/1JZX7Mi

*All Pepped Up* (Pepper Jones #2): http://amzn.to/1UzIIpL

*Pepped Up & Ready* (Pepper Jones #3): http://amzn.to/1UzIIpL

*Pep Talks* (Pepper Jones #4): http://amzn.to/1Ph79EI

*Pepped Up Forever* (Pepper Jones #5): http://amzn.to/1VR7nW2

*The Pepper Jones Collection* (first three books in the series): http://amzn.to/1L2GGVA

# Acknowledgements

I've never done a long-winded acknowledgement at the end of a book because I figured that it was more important to let the people who've helped me know how much I appreciate it without having to read to the end of one of my books! But you know, why not shout out these people's praises to the whole world, or at least those people who read my book and continue to the acknowledgements section? So here we go.

I'll start with my amazing husband. I love reading and writing books that have strong romance themes, but it's not because I'm filling a void missing in my life. Actually, it's the opposite. I have my own little fantasy and love story with my husband, and I just want everyone to get a little happily-ever-after in their lives. Even if it's fictional. So yeah, thanks to my husband for, in part, letting me know just what an awesome, healthy and loving relationship looks like. It makes it way easier to write about falling in love when I've got you as a perfect example. I'm not used to being so cheesy but hey, that's the point of this section, isn't it?

I definitely want to shout out to my older sister who is basically my cheerleader. She encourages me in everything in my life and especially in my writing.

I'm super blessed to have found my editor, Leanne, who has helped me from the very beginning in figuring out how to write a compelling story. She is wicked smart and the comments she leaves as she edits often make me burst out laughing (earning me strange looks from those at the coffee shop).

I also have to thank Ashley who wears lots of hats: my publicist, beta reader, plot-sounding-board, and um, coach? She whips me into shape when I start to get off track/go on reading binges instead of writing my own books, and she makes sure I don't stray (too far) from my deadlines.

And Theresa, my cover-artist/teammate in writing. She put up with my indecision about what I wanted to do for the covers for this series and I'm so happy with how they turned out!

Lastly, my readers are the biggest force behind my desire to keep writing books and creating characters. It will never cease to amaze me that the things on my heart and in my head can translate into stories that impact others, and I love hearing back from you guys when one of my stories makes a difference in your life. I want to keep writing books that make you happy.

CPSIA information can be obtained
at www.ICGtesting.com
Printed in the USA
FSHW021320110520
70129FS

9 781530 919536